RETURN TO SULA

By the same author in Pan Books

SULA

RETURN TO SULA

LAVINIA DERWENT

Cover illustration by Prudence Seward

Text illustration by Louise Annand

A Piccolo Book

PAN BOOKS LTD

LONDON AND SYDNEY

First published 1971 by Victor Gollancz Ltd
This edition published 1974 by Pan Books Ltd,
Cavaye Place, London SW10 9PG

ISBN 0 330 24173 7

Printed in Great Britain by
Richard Clay (The Chaucer Press), Ltd, Bungay, Suffolk

CONTENTS

Chapter 1

HOME TO SULA

The young seals were playing hide-and-seek in the cold Atlantic water. Or was it follow-my-leader? They frisked about like children, letting out excited little cries as their sleek bodies twisted and turned beneath the waves.

Sometimes only their heads could be seen bobbing above the water. Sometimes they took brave backward leaps, trying to turn somersaults. Sometimes the surf splashed them nearer to the shore.

They would wriggle about on the sand for a short time, then flop back into the sea. Always they kept a wary eye on Old Whiskers, sunning himself like a sentinel on a nearby rock.

The old seal was past taking part in such frolics. He gave a grunt as he watched the water-babies at play. Silly young things! Could they not be content to keep still? What he liked best was to lie drowsing in the sun, feeling the warmth seeping through his skin, and listening to the cry of the sea-birds circling overhead.

Old Whiskers shifted his body along the rock, seeking for his lost companion. What had become of the boy? Magnus had been missing for days. Or was it weeks? The old seal felt lost without him, lying there on his own. He lifted his head and gazed around him, hoping for a sight of the familiar figure leaping lightly across the rocks. He could see the row of houses at the harbour, but no eager boy running along the sand. For the first time in his life, Magnus had deserted him.

A dark shadow crept across the sun. The old seal shivered. He gave a snuffling sigh and slid off the rock into the water. It was not the same without the boy. Would he never come back?

Magnus Macduff was already on his way back, as fast as the *Hebridean* could carry him. But not fast enough.

'Hurry up! Hurry up!' he told the ship, longing for a first sight of Sula. 'Get a move on!'

The old ship did her best. She put on a spurt of speed and lurched round Sula Point, escorted by a formation of screaming gulls. They passed and re-passed each other, diving down now and again to pick up crusts of bread floating on the water. The successful ones made off like lightning, hastily swallowing their titbit before it could be snatched from their beaks.

Their raucous cries sounded like sweet music to the boy's ears. He hung over the rails, envying them their wings. If only he could be airborne he would not waste time swooping down into the water. He would make straight for Sula, the little island that lay ahead.

Calum Campbell, the skipper, was calling down to him from the bridge.

'You'll be glad to get home, Magnus?'

'Uh-huh!'

It was the biggest understatement Magnus had ever made. Glad to get home! His heart was thumping like a steam-engine. But he was not one to express his feelings in words, to the captain or anyone else. Not that there were many people on board. Only the crew and a couple of strangers.

They were young men with flaxen hair and reddish beards, wearing shorts and shaggy stockings, and carrying rucksacks on their backs. Bird-watchers, maybe, or just tourists. Magnus had heard them tell the captain that they came from Scandinavia. They were difficult to tell apart, except that one wore a blue and the other a red tammy. The best thing about them was that they kept themselves to themselves.

The ship was creaking like an old woman with rheumaticky joints. 'Get on, you!' Magnus shouted within himself. 'Hurry up!'

He gazed up at the sea-birds waltzing overhead. There was one more graceful and less greedy than the others. A fulmar floating on the air without beating its wings. How could it stay up like that? The boy's fingers itched for a pencil so that he could draw a picture of the bird. He stored up the details in his mind's eye. Later, he would put them down on paper, perhaps on the margin of one of his schoolbooks. It would be great to be back in the island schoolroom again, little though he liked lessons.

More and more birds were flying out from the rocks and crags to greet the ship. The air was thick with gulls, gannets, guillemots, terns and razor-bills. It was a friendly welcome, an air-display that warmed the boy's heart.

'Sula ahead!'

Magnus gave an inward whoop of joy. There it was, just as he had left it: Sula, 'the gannet rock' standing sturdily in the sea, with Little Sula away to the west. There was nothing beyond, except America – the United States, as far out of reach as the moon. But Sula was the only place in the world that mattered.

Magnus had feared that it might have changed behind his back, but it was still the same. The Heathery Hill was in its usual place. So was the church and the school and the little row of houses at the harbour. Even the stunted rowan tree in the Manse garden was still leaning at the same angle.

Three blasts from the ship's siren. When they heard the signal, the people came flocking down to the pier. They were only shapes in the distance, yet Magnus could put names to them all without straining his eyes.

'There's Gran!'

He felt a lump in his throat as he recognized Gran's upright figure striding down to the jetty in her shapeless garments. He had not realized how fond he was of the old woman until he left the island. It must be true what they said about absence making the heart grow fonder. He waved to her, but Gran did not wave back. She was not one for showing her feelings any more than he was. He would never know whether her heart had grown fonder.

He scanned the water, hoping for a glimpse of Old Whiskers. Yet he knew the seal would have more sense than to show himself with so many people about. Wait till the stir had settled, and they would get together. They would lie on the rock, side by side, and then Magnus would know he had really come home.

The people were more distinct now. He could see Mrs Gillies, the District Nurse, leaning on her bicycle. The minister, the Reverend Alexander Morrison, was waving his hat as if giving three hearty cheers. Andrew Murray, the schoolmaster, was limping down to the harbour with his little dog at his heels; and Jinty Cowan was prancing with excitement at the water's edge. She was wearing a blue bow in her hair. She was a great one for dressing up, especially if she wanted to attract attention. And Jinty's main object in life was to attract Magnus.

They were all there, even Mr Skinnymalink, the lone Hermit, hiding in the background. Unlike Jinty, he had no desire to be noticed. He waited till he saw that the boy was on board, then he loped away back to his lonely hut. He was content, knowing that Magnus would seek him out later on.

Angus Alastair McCallum, known as Tair, was standing on his head taking an upside-down look at the ship, while the Ferret was picking up a handful of pebbles to use as ammunition for his catapult. Magnus on board would make a good target.

Magnus flexed his muscles as his gaze focused on his sparring-partner. He could do with a good fight after the easy-osy life he had been leading on the mainland. It would be a pleasure to punch the Ferret's nose.

'Hullo, Magnus! It's great to see you!' Jinty's shrill voice carried across the water. 'Oh my! you look just the same.' She sounded surprised, as if she had expected him to be changed from his contact with the outside world.

Suddenly he felt shy and ill-at-ease standing there in his good suit with everyone looking at him. He wanted to get off the boat without any fuss, to feel the good soil of Sula beneath his feet, get rid of his Sunday clothes and rush off to find Old Whiskers. But they were all crowding round the gangway asking questions.

'How did you get on, Magnus?'

'What was the town like?'

'Did you see the sights?'

'Are you pleased to be back?'

Magnus answered only the last question. 'Uh-huh!' It was as much as he was prepared to say at the moment. Gran did not say anything. She just looked at him and gave a little nod. Magnus nodded back, and that was that.

Luckily, the two tourists appeared, and all attention was riveted on them. Even Jinty's. Magnus took the chance to push his way through the crowd. He ran zigzag up to the row of little houses, and dived in at Gran's open door. Refuge! He was back home.

Gran had been baking. The scones and oatcakes were propped up on a wire tray on the table. Pancakes, too, which Gran called drop-scones, and a dark treacly gingerbread which she made only on special occasions. Was it a welcome-home treat?

Magnus's mouth watered at the sight of it, and at the frying-pan waiting by the side of the fire. This was

the night of the big feed, when the *Hebridean* brought
supplies from the mainland as a change from the customary plain fare. Soon there would be kippers fry-
ing and sausages sizzling in every cottage kitchen. For
those who could afford it, there would be butcher's
meat, baker's cakes with icing on them, bananas and
oranges. It was always a hunger or a burst.

Magnus could wait for his meal. He had better things
to do than eat. He ran up the steep stairs to his bedroom, where everything was cool and neat and bare.
No rugs, no curtains, no ornaments; nothing to clutter
it up and take away from its breathing-space. Best of all
was the view from the window, down to the harbour
and across the sea to Little Sula.

In less than two minutes he was in his old patched
trousers and darned jersey. Bare-footed, he rushed out
into the fresh air, taking great gulps as he ran.

'Hooray!' he shouted to himself. 'I'm back!'

He felt richer than any millionaire. The *Hebridean*
was already backing out of the pier like a clumsy cart-
horse. 'Thank goodness I'm not on board,' thought
Magnus, slithering across the seaweed. He was making
for his own special rock and a meeting with the seal.

In the pools he could see the delicate colours of
anemones floating in the water, waving their frills as
they twisted and turned. Hermit crabs, shrimps, and
little nameless fishes caught his eye; but he hurried on.
He would see them all later. He could not waste another
moment before being reunited with Old Whiskers.

'Where's Magnus?'

Everyone seemed to be looking for him, except Gran

and Mr Skinnymalink, who had more sense. The Hermit was back in his solitary hut polishing away at the stones of Sula. Gran was having a word with the tourists, asking if they needed shelter for the night. The old woman was gruff, but in her own way hospitable.

'No, thank you. You are most kind.'

The two heads, in their blue and red tammies, bowed politely. They had a tent, the men told her, and sleeping-bags. But perhaps the kind lady would supply them with milk.

Gran gave a brief nod. They followed her as she tramped up to her door and waited outside till she brought them milk and a sample of her baking.

'How much, please?' they asked, fumbling in their pockets for money.

'We'll settle up later,' Gran told them. She was tough, but not mean. Nor did she ask why they were here or how long they were staying. Everyone had a right to their own secrets.

The Ferret followed them stealthily. He watched as they pitched their small tent at the foot of the Heathery Hill. It would make a good target for a catapult. He would wait till the strangers were settled inside, and then let fly with his chuckie-stone. It would pass the time till he could have a fight with Magnus.

Jinty watched, too, re-tying her blue ribbon into a bigger bow. It was something to do until Magnus showed up. She had a good idea where he was. It had taken all her powers of restraint not to follow him. 'Wait,' she warned herself. 'You might catch him when he comes back. He's always in a better mood, after he's seen the seal.'

*

They were together at last, the boy and the seal, stretched out on the rock in perfect harmony. Old Whiskers nuzzled his wet snout against the boy's neck and gave little grunts of satisfaction. Magnus's arms were flung across the seal's body, keeping him close by his side. This was his heaven. The seal, the salty air, the whirr of birds' wings overhead. He was home.

'Never again!' he vowed, snuggling closer to Old Whiskers. 'I'll never leave Sula again.'

Chapter 2

THE WINNING PRIZE

It had begun as an ordinary enough day. Magnus was sitting in his usual place in the schoolroom overlooking the harbour. He was drawing a picture of a bumble-bee in the margin of his reading-book. The book was about a horse called Black Beauty.

Every blank space in the book was already covered with pictures of crabs and gulls and seals. Black Beauty was there, too, drawn in a dozen different positions.

The bee was easy enough to draw. A real bumble-bee had flown in through the window, and was buzzing around the blackboard as if trying to add up the sums. Magnus had noted every detail before committing them to paper. Furry body, long tongue, black-and-yellow stripes. Every single item in his drawing was in the correct proportion.

The bee was the only one paying any attention to the sums. The handful of pupils, all at different ages and stages, were taking advantage of the fact that the teacher's eye was off them. Andrew Murray was busy reading a letter that lay on his desk. They had more sense than to work when he wasn't looking.

Tair was talking to Avizandum, his familiar who lived in his pocket. Nobody else could see Avizandum, but he was more real to Tair than all the people in Sula put together. Avizandum knew everything. He was Tair's very best friend.

Red Sandy and Black Sandy were having a competition to see how far they could stick their tongues out at each other. Jinty Cowan was trying to tempt Magnus with a liquorice-allsort from a paper bag.

'Go on, Magnus. Choose which one you want. You can have two, if you like.'

'No, thanks.'

The Ferret accepted the invitation instead. He snatched a sweet and swallowed it in one gulp, like a greedy gull. 'Let's have another,' he said, and made a swoop at the paper bag.

'You wait till you're asked,' said Jinty primly, and hid the bag in her pocket.

The Ferret made a face at her, and then began to buzz, copying the bee. It was something to do. He changed gear now and again, as he pretended to zoom round the classroom.

'What are you doing, boy?' The teacher looked up and spoke to the Ferret in a sharp voice.

'Nothing, sir.'

'Then, stop it at once.'

'Yessir.'

The Ferret stopped, but he felt bereft. There was a gap to fill. What could he do instead? Dip Jinty's pigtails into the inkwell? Make more blotting-paper pellets for his catapult? Stick a pin into Tair? Sort out the grubby contents of his pocket?

None of these ideas appealed to him. Then suddenly the bee came bumbling towards him like an over-laden aeroplane. That was it! The Ferret sat up, having found a new purpose in life. He would catch the bee and stick it down the neck of one of the girls, just for the fun of hearing her squeal. Or maybe he could find a wee bottle and put the bee inside. Or he could watch it drown in the inkwell. There were plently of ploys he could try.

Magnus happened to look up from his drawing and guessed what was in the Ferret's mind.

'Stop it, you!' he hissed, and gave the Ferret a dunt on the back.

'You mind your own business.' The Ferret whirled round with his fists clenched. 'I'll punch your nose.'

'Away!' scoffed Magnus. 'I'll smash yours to smithereens.'

The Ferret picked up the nearest weapon – his wooden ruler – and took a lunge at Magnus. Magnus dodged, then grabbed his own ruler and was ready for the fray. The fencing-match went on in deadly earnest. Parry and thrust. Hit and miss. No rules to the game.

It was not easy to fight silently. The contestants tried to control their grunts and groans in case the teacher heard. But it was difficult not to cry out when a weapon was rammed against the gullet. Andrew Murray looked up with a frown when a strangled cry escaped from the Ferret's lips.

'Stop it at once,' he rapped out.

The boys subsided, but the teacher did not take his

eye off them. He got up from his desk and limped towards them.

'You should be ashamed of yourselves,' he said sternly.

'Yessir,' agreed the Ferret. He put on his best ashamed act, slouching down in his seat with a look of abject sorrow on his face. It was a comic effort, meant to rouse a titter in the class. But Magnus did not change his expression. He felt no shame, except that he had not hit the Ferret harder.

'Come out, Magnus.'

The teacher walked back to his desk and waited for Magnus to follow him. The others sat up, sensing drama.

'Mercy me!' gasped Jinty Cowan. She went pink and then white with worry. Surely Magnus was not going to be punished merely for not looking ashamed? Old Miss Macfarlane, their previous teacher, would just have said, 'Tut-tut,' and left it at that. But the new man, though they were getting used to his ways, was a bit funny at times.

She stretched out her neck to see if the dreaded leather strap was lying on the teacher's desk. The hangman's whip. She breathed a sigh of relief. There was nothing there except a letter, the one the teacher had been reading so intently.

The others sat gaping, hoping for something exciting to happen. Avizandum whispered a warning to Tair: 'Look out! Watch yourself!'

'Yes, I will,' Tair whispered back, and sat with folded arms, looking as if butter would not melt in his mouth.

The class was in for a disappointment. Nothing happened. Even the bumble-bee deserted them and flew dizzily out of the open window. 'Get on with your work,' the teacher said sharply. Then he turned to Magnus and spoke to him in such a soft voice that even Jinty's sharp ears could not catch a word.

'Look at this, Magnus.' Andrew Murray showed him a paper on the desk with a letter lying beside it.

Magnus looked. So what? It was only a piece of paper. The *Hebridean* had brought in the mail yesterday. Some of the islanders had received letters and postcards and newspapers. Even Gran, though it was unusual for her to have any correspondence. Magnus could not see the point of people always writing to each other, saying they had no news, that the weather was so-so, and they must stop now, hoping that everybody was keeping well.

The teacher's letter had a more official look about it.

'You remember that competition, Magnus?' he asked, looking at his pupil.

'What?' said Magnus vaguely.

'The drawing competition,' said Andrew Murray with a note of impatience in his voice. Talking to Magnus was like holding a conversation with a stone dyke. Yet he held himself in check. If there was one thing he had learned since coming to Sula, it was that Magnus was not to be driven.

This was Andrew's second summer in Sula. He had come here for his health's sake, to replace old Miss Macfarlane, but he was finding more than renewed strength. He was becoming self-reliant, like the islanders themselves.

Everyone in Sula had to fall back on their own re-
sources. They had to be their own cobbler, dyker,
crofter, fisherman – and many another thing besides.
Even the children could turn their hands to a variety
of tasks. They could mend nets, gut fish, dig peat, build
dykes, climb up the craggy rocks in search of sea-
birds' eggs, and take their turn at manning the boats.
Their knowledge of nature was far ahead of the
teacher's. It was a different matter when it came to
learning from lesson-books.

Old Miss Macfarlane had been easy-going. She had
shut her eyes to their shortcomings and let them play
truant when they liked. Andrew had tightened the
reins, with some success. Jinty Cowan was his brightest
pupil. Too bright at times. Little Miss Know-All was
always the first to shoot up her hand.

'Please, sir, I know the answer, sir.'

Magnus, on the other hand, had little to say for himself. Yet it was he who was the most outstanding pupil,
in the teacher's opinion. Not only because he had a
strange magic at his finger-tips and could make a minnow or a mouse live with a few deft strokes of his pencil. There was also a deep-down quality in the boy
which Andrew admired. But how to reach it? The way
to Magnus's heart was as tortuous as a maze.

All the same, the teacher felt he was making progress.
Otherwise, how could he have persuaded the boy to
enter the competition in the first place?

It had happened months ago. 'Magnus, will you
do me a favour?' he began, approaching the subject
warily.

'I might.'

So far, so good. Andrew's next move was to lay a new drawing-book on the boy's desk.

'I'd like you to draw a special picture.'

'What for?' asked Magnus suspiciously.

'Well, actually, it's for a competition.'

Magnus gave the schoolmaster one of his looks. 'No, thanks,' he said flatly. Competition of any kind did not come into his scheme of living.

Andrew knew better than to coax him. 'Oh, well, it doesn't matter. It was just an idea. You can get on with your reading instead. How are you enjoying *Black Beauty*?'

'It's not bad.'

Left to himself, Magnus began to turn over the pages. The story was interesting enough. Better than the rubbish old Miss Macfarlane made him read, about fairies and gnomes, and Henny-Penny going to market with her silly shopping-basket. All the same, reading any book was a slow job. Words were clumsy things compared to pictures.

Now and then his eyes roamed from the printed page to the new drawing-book on his desk. He had never had so much blank paper at his disposal before. It would be a pity not to use it.

Magnus pushed *Black Beauty* aside and picked up a pencil. Andrew Murray watched him and smiled with secret satisfaction. His tactics had been right. It was best to leave the boy alone and await results.

The stir of the classroom went on around him, but Magnus did not hear it. He shut his ears to Kirsty lisping out her poetry.

Wee Willy Winky runth through the toon,

Upthtairth and doonthtairth in hith nightgoon ...

He did not listen to Jinty saying in a smug voice, 'Please, sir, I've finished my sums.' Or Tair having a fit of giggles at some comic remark of Avizandum's. He did not even notice that the Ferret was bombarding him with inky pellets. He just brushed them off and went on drawing.

It was strange starting on a blank page instead of trying to find space on a margin. For a moment he hesitated, then his pencil began to move. There was no trouble finding subjects to draw. The seals, and the wild life of Sula were his favourite studies.

He roughed in a picture of Old Whiskers lying on the rock with the young seals frisking around him in the water. Then he filled in the background with sea-birds. Gulls, guillemots, gannets and terns swooped through the air. A pair of puffins pecked at their feathers on a nearby ledge, and a razor-bill sharpened its beak on a rocky stone.

The boy had made a careful study of feathers, beaks, wings and claws. He knew the span of each bird's wing, the correct angle at which it would turn and swoop, the way a claw curled or an eye swivelled. Every detail was exact. But the picture was not static. Magnus had given it movement.

Old Whiskers seemed to be breathing in and out as he lay supine upon the rock. The young seals were turning somersaults. The birds flew across the page. The sea swished in to the shore.

Magnus was putting the final touch to a clump of sea-pinks when he was suddenly aware of a draught of hot air on his neck. It was Jinty, breathing heavily. She had finished her sums and was now looking for fresh kingdoms to conquer.

'Draw me, Magnus,' she invited him, though she knew fine it would be a miracle if he did.

'Away!' said Magnus, hiding the drawing with his arm. Now that it was finished, he did not want anyone to see it. Least of all the teacher who appeared at his side and said, 'Let me look, Magnus.'

Magnus reluctantly withdrew his arm. The teacher let out a cry of admiration. 'That's it! It's a splendid picture. Give it to me, Magnus, please. I'll send it in for the competition.'

Magnus glowered at him. For two pins he would have torn the drawing into little pieces – seals, seagulls and all. Still, there were plenty of blank pages left. He could easily draw more pictures when he was alone, and keep them to himself. If the man was so keen on this one, let him have it.

'Okay!' he said, and gave Andrew a take-it-or-leave-it look.

'Sign your name at the foot,' said Andrew, pleased with his success.

Magnus could draw a bird or a fish with a few deft strokes. But writing was a painful process, even something as familiar as his own name. He chewed his tongue and pressed the pencil clumsily on the paper. Anyone seeing his squiggled signature would have a poor opinion of the writer, but if they looked at the drawing they would have no doubts where his talent lay.

When the teacher had taken the drawing away, Magnus sat back ready to turn his attention to other matters.

The Ferret was aiming his catapult at him. Right! The time had come for revenge.

He dived below the desk and crawled towards the enemy. The Ferret squirmed in his seat and kicked out, but it was no use. Magnus gripped his legs and held them firm while he tied the boy's bootlaces together in tight knots. Wait till the Ferret got up and tried to walk home!

Now, months later, the teacher was telling Magnus in an excited voice, 'You've won first prize.'

'Mercy me.'

Magnus felt a faint thrill of pleasure, more for the man's sake than his own. Andrew Murray seemed to be bursting with pride. In a way, the success was his.

'Look, Magnus. You'll have to choose. Which prize would you like?'

There were pictures of the prizes lying on the desk. First, a split-new bicycle, the latest model. Magnus looked at it without any desire to own it. He had his feet, hadn't he? If he wanted a ride on a bicycle he could always use the rickety old bone-shaker discarded by the District Nurse. It was communal property, propped up against a rusty bath-tub at the back of the Cowans' cottage. It had been taken apart a dozen times and put together again, just for fun. Mrs Gillies had a new bicycle now, but even so she sometimes used the old one. 'I feel more attached to it,' she declared.

The next prize was a cheque, but once more Magnus showed no interest in it. He did not even look at the amount of money. It might be a fortune for all he cared. What would he do with a fortune? It could not buy him the things he liked best. Freedom to lie in the sun beside Old Whiskers, to watch a bird building its nest, or see how a frog blew itself up. The things he enjoyed most were free.

The third prize was a box of paints with strange names : rose-madder, cobalt blue, green bice, Chinese white, yellow ochre. They were all new to Magnus. Maybe if he mixed them up he could find the right colour for a puffin's beak, or the subtle shadings of a seal, or the chalky-white of a gannet's egg, and the pale purple bloom of a heather-bell.

In his mind's eye he could see pages of his drawing-book filled with scarlet rowan-berries, burnt-brown bracken, and the pale pinks and blues of a Sula sky at sunrise.

'Well, have you made up your mind?' asked the teacher.

'Yes.' Magnus looked up at him. 'I'd like the box of paints.'

'Right!' So far so good. Andrew was not sure of his next move. He looked at the letter on his desk. How could he tell Magnus what Mr John Craigie, the Art Master at Cronan High School, had written?

'You've got a young genius on your hands, Andrew. I only wish I had him on mine! Tell him to come across and collect his prize. I'd like to have a look at him and discuss his future. Send him across to Cronan as soon as possible.'

Send Magnus! It would be as easy to pick Little Sula out of the sea and post it to the mainland in a brown paper parcel. Easier!

Andrew could not think of a subtle enough approach.

'You've never been across to Cronan, Magnus?' he asked, knowing full well what the answer would be.

Magnus shook his head without bothering to reply. He was still thinking of mixing burnt sienna with ultramarine and seeing if it might match a kingfisher's feather.

'Do you ever think of taking a trip to the mainland?' asked Andrew, floundering in deep water.

'No!'

The teacher sighed, and made a final effort. 'It might be a good idea if you went, Magnus. Mr Craigie, the Art Master at the High School, is very anxious to see you. In fact, he suggests that you should go across to collect your prize. Then you could have a talk with him about your – er – future.'

Magnus gave him a cool look. What was the man talking about? Fancy leaving Sula just for the sake of collecting a prize and having a 'talk' with an unknown art master!

'No thanks, I'll not bother about the prize,' he said, and turned away to go back to his place. Never mind the madders and magentas and indigo blues. The price was too high to pay. He could get on fine with a plain pencil.

It was not the first time Andrew Murray had been left high and dry. He sat at his desk staring at the letter and puzzling out his problem. He could not insist on Magnus going to Cronan. Better leave the boy alone, and push the problem aside for the moment. Something might happen.

Something had happened already. There was a knock at the door. The children sat up expectantly, welcoming any diversion. Perhaps it was the Reverend Alexander Morrison come to give them a Bible lesson. It would be better than doing sums. The minister was a daft man, always making silly jokes and drawing funny faces on the blackboard. Sometimes he told them stories about the Good Samaritan and the Prodigal Son, and had a great time to himself acting out the parts. He could fairly let himself go at Daniel in the Lion's Den.

'Come in,' called the teacher.

The children gasped with surprise when they saw who entered, Magnus more than any. He could not believe his eyes. It was not the Reverend Morrison. It was Gran.

What on earth was *she* doing here, in her old working clothes, with a man's cap on her head and tackety boots on her feet? Not that Magnus felt ashamed of her. She was just Gran, the way she always looked. What puzzled him was why she had come. She had a letter in her hand, the one which had arrived yesterday with the *Hebridean*.

'Can you spare a moment, Mr Murray?' she asked in a loud whisper, tip-toeing towards him in her clumsy boots. She need not have worried about disturbing the children. They had no intention of working while Gran was there.

'Yes, of course, Mrs Macduff.' Andrew rose to greet her. 'What can I do for you?'

She laid the letter on his desk. As the teacher read it, the children made wild guesses as to its contents. The Ferret had a bright idea. 'She's been left a fortune. She's asking the teacher if we can get a half-holiday.'

Jinty had an even better thought. 'It's from the

Queen. Her Majesty's coming to Sula for her summer holidays. Gran'll have to curtsey.'

The thought of Gran curtseying set everybody giggling, except Tair. He was listening to Avizandum, whispering from his pocket. 'Mark my words, it's something to do with Magnus.'

So it was. Gran and the teacher were taking quick looks in Magnus's direction. Finally they heard Andrew say, with an uncertain note in his voice, 'Leave it to me, Mrs Macduff. I'll have a word with him, but you know what Magnus is like. I doubt if he'll go.'

Chapter 3

ACROSS TO CRONAN

It was not Gran's letter that did the trick. Nor the thought of a fine new paint-box awaiting Magnus in Cronan. It was Rory, old Cowan's collie-dog.

Rory was a tough, hard-working beast. At a whistle from his master he would round up Bilko the goat, chase after a wandering cow, or run to the top of the Heathery Hill to bring down a stray sheep. He went out in the boat, too, standing still and steady in the prow like a figure-head carved out of wood.

Though he belonged to old Cowan he was everybody's dog, part of the island scene. Like Specky the hen or Gran's aspidistra, he was always there. When he was off-duty he lay outside the Cowans' door, keeping one eye open for any passer-by. Magnus always had a word with him, man-to-man, never talking down to him in doggy language.

'It's a fine day, Rory. Coming for a walk?'

The dog was up like a shot, ready and willing; and the two would set off side-by-side in companionable silence. Rory did not need constant patting and petting. Like Magnus, he could keep himself to himself.

But lately something had gone wrong with the dog. Magnus had first noticed it one day when he was out digging peat. Rory was rounding up some straggling ewes, gathering them together into a little group. He went down on his belly, keeping the sheep under control by the power of the eye. Then he got up and crept cautiously forward. Suddenly the dog seemed to waver, and walked slap-bang into a fence. He staggered for a moment, then shook himself and righted his direction.

'What's up, Rory?' Magnus went forward to speak to him.

The dog gazed up at him with a glazed look in his eye. Then he hung his head and lay down at the boy's feet. Magnus caught his breath. Surely not that! Could Rory be going blind?

Magnus felt sure of it as he watched the dog's movements during the next few days. He saw the collie stumble over a pail which Gran had set down while feeding the hens. He watched Rory wander off in the wrong direction when old Cowan whistled to him. Then one day he saw him getting in the way of the District Nurse's bicycle, narrowly escaping being run over.

He tried his best to shield the dog, hoping no one else would notice. He went with Rory to bring in the goat and to round up the sheep. 'Keep close by me, Rory. It'll be all right,' said the boy soothingly. But, of course, the day came when the dog was found out.

It was the District Nurse again who brought matters

to a head. She came wobbling off her bicycle one day when Rory strayed across her path. Mrs Gillies landed on one leg and said crossly, 'Watch where you're going, you silly thing.' Then, taking a closer look at the dog, her voice softened. 'What's wrong, Rory? Are you ill?'

If Rory had been a human being she would have been in her element. An epidemic would have raised her spirits sky-high. But at the moment her only patient was Jinty Cowan who had come out in spots. Mrs Gillies had been hopeful that it might turn out to be measles, at least. But it was only the result of eating too many sweets.

'I've got a pain in my pinny,' whined Jinty, feeling sorry for herself and wanting attention as usual.

'Serves you right,' said the District Nurse. 'Stuffing yourself with caramels. You'll ruin your complexion as well as your stomach. Open your mouth and swallow your medicine. A fine film-star you'll make, all covered with pimples.'

Jinty had already decided on her career. She was to be a film-star. A leading-lady dressed in glamorous garments. The hero – bearing a strong likeness to Magnus – would bend over to kiss her lily-white hand, murmuring, 'Darling, I love you.' Music! Fade!

Meantime, she consoled herself with liquorice-allsorts and chocolate caramels.

Magnus was near at hand when the District Nurse spoke to the dog. So was old Cowan. Magnus heard Mrs Gillies saying, 'What's wrong with Rory?'

The boy's heart turned over when he heard the answer. 'He's done for, I doubt. The dog's been going blind for weeks. I'll have to destroy him.'

Magnus went white with rage. He rushed at old Cowan, clenching his fists and shouting, 'You'll not destroy him! I'll kill *you* first! You're a cruel man!'

Old Cowan was no more cruel than anyone else, but he was a practical man. 'Hold on, Magnus,' he said mildly. 'A working dog's no use if he can't see where he's going. It would be the kindest thing to put him out of his misery. After all, he's just a dog.'

Just a dog! Magnus glared angrily at old Cowan. Rory was much more than a dog; he was a member of the community. Magnus had drawn his picture a hundred times, and shared countless expeditions with him up the Heathery Hill and across to Little Sula. He was a friend, not 'just a dog'.

The boy turned in despair to the District Nurse. 'Could you not do something, Mrs Gillies?' he pleaded. 'Could you not cure him?'

'Well now,' began Mrs Gillies, unwilling to admit failure, 'it's really a job for a vet.' She had often patched up paws and extracted thorns, but curing blindness was another matter.

She stooped to take a closer look at the collie, who blinked up at her. 'Cataract, most likely. Archie would be the man. Archie Tosh, the vet at Cronan. He's good with dogs.'

'Well, then!' cried Magnus, feeling a great load falling off his back. He turned to old Cowan. 'Couldn't you take him across to the vet?'

Old Cowan snapped his braces. 'Me! I've got more to do than career across to Cronan, what with the hay and the peat and the fishing and everything. It would be easier to get another dog.'

The load landed back on the boy's shoulders with a
heavy thud, but he tried again. 'Maybe somebody else
could go?'

He looked hopefully at the District Nurse, but she
was kicking her bicycle-pedal into place ready to re-
mount. 'Not me! You'd all be down with the mumps
the minute I left.' She hoisted herself into the saddle
and rode away, calling back, 'What about going yourself, Magnus?'

So here he was, on board the *Hebridean*, sailing away
from Sula for the first time in his life, dressed in his
best suit, with the dog at his heels.

Magnus never felt comfortable in his best suit. For
years it had been too big for him. Now it was too small.
The trousers were tight, the jacket nipped him under
the arms, the waistcoat would not button unless he
pulled himself in and held his breath. The whole outfit
had an old-fashioned look about it, but at least it had
one thing in its favour. It was cut down from his
father's Sunday suit.

He had few momentos of the man who had been lost
in a storm off Sula Point. Even fewer memories of his
mother who had died soon afterwards, of a broken
heart, they said. The fact that his father had once worn
the same suit was some compensation to Magnus for
its discomfort.

Old Morag McCallum, who acted as tailor on the
island, had made it, sewing it with everlasting stitches
which held together in spite of stresses and strains. The
buttons were on for life, and the cloth itself – of good
Harris tweed – would never wear out.

There were two letters in his breast-pocket. One was from the schoolmaster addressed to John Craigie, D.A., Art Master, Cronan High School. The other was the letter Gran had received. But they were not important. It was Rory who mattered.

Nothing else would have made Magnus leave the island, even for one short week. Short! It loomed ahead like a lifetime as he stood on deck watching the group gathered on the shore growing smaller and smaller. Jinty was still waving a tearful farewell, like a tragic heroine. Gran was shading her eyes. The Ferret was having a last fling with his catapult – but soon they would all fade from sight.

The homesick feeling struck Magnus even before the ship rounded the point. If it had not been for Rory he would have dived overboard and set out for the shore, tight trousers and all. The dog seemed to sense that he had found a saviour. For the last few days he had scarcely left the boy's side. Now he sat on deck, feeling secure as long as Magnus was near him. When the boy moved, the dog moved with him.

Sula faded from sight. The gulls screamed a last sad farewell. There was nothing to watch now except the wake in the water.

'What about a cup of tea, Magnus?' Captain Campbell's voice boomed out from the bridge. The man was trying to be kind. 'Go down and help yourself. They've got doughnuts.'

Magnus shook his head. He could not swallow the lump in his throat, let alone a doughnut. He roamed restlessly round the deck with Rory at his heels, looking over the rails at each side. Then he went and sat like a displaced person on a coil of rope.

The dog licked his hand and gave a whine. 'It's okay, Rory; don't worry,' said Magnus, not sure which one was comforting the other. The bond between them seemed to grow stronger. They were both suffering.

At last the *Hebridean* slid into Cronan harbour. Magnus stared in surprise. There seemed to be hundreds and thousands of people on the quayside, all restlessly coming and going. Not a soul standing still. The boy had never heard such a din. Even the sea-birds screamed at a higher pitch – town-birds rather than island-birds.

Magnus looked beyond the harbour up towards the town. The houses were all jammed together, some built on top of each other, reaching several stories high. What a way to live, crowded like sardines in a tin.

'Are you coming, Magnus?'

Captain Campbell wanted to take him straight to Rockview, the boarding-house where the boy was to stay. It was run by Mrs Reekie, a cousin of the Cowans. She had been cook at Cronan Castle before Willy Reekie married her, or, more truthfully, before she married Willy Reekie. He was too meek and mild to make up his own mind. Most of the day he was out, working at the Forestry. When he came home, he was content to sink into a chair and let his wife rule the roost.

All this Magnus had still to find out. Meantime he said a firm 'No' to Captain Campbell. 'I'm going to take Rory to the vet first.'

'Please yourself, Magnus.' Captain Campbell had plenty of other matters on his mind. 'You'll find the vet's place in the High Street. Straight ahead. Number sixty-five. Mrs Reekie's place is just round the corner. I'll take a look-in to see you some time during the week.'

'Thanks, Mr Campbell. Ch-Cheerio.'

Magnus walked down the gangway with the dog stumbling behind him. It was like walking into a whirlwind, with so much noise and confusion all around. It jarred on his ears and grew louder as he neared the High Street. He wanted to tone it down; to put on the soft pedal. How could anyone think or feel in such a medley?

The rain was coming down in a steady drizzle, as if someone had forgotten to turn off the tap. At home Magnus would have taken no notice of it, apart from maybe putting an old sack over his head. But here the folk seemed to make a great fuss about the weather. Even the men carried umbrellas, and everyone wore waterproofs. Magnus took little notice of the people or the shops or the traffic. He made straight for his target. Number sixty-five, High Street.

He found A. TOSH, VET. SURGEON next door to a pet shop. Magnus stared in at the window, not believing his eyes. He had never seen living creatures shut up like this before. Little white mice were running frenzied races round a turning treadmill, never getting anywhere. Sometimes they tumbled off and bravely jumped on again. Why were they doing it? For fun, or to break the monotony of captivity?

Magnus longed to set them free to run a straighter race in the fresh air. He wanted to draw them, too, as they turned forward somersaults or took valiant leaps

into the air. He could have watched them all day, unaware of the jostling passers-by.

There were other living creatures in the window.
Cages full of brightly coloured birds such as he had
never seen in Sula. They twittered to each other, keeping up an endless conversation. A black-and-white
rabbit was nibbling a limp piece of lettuce. A Persian
cat snoozed with her head between her paws. Goldfish
swam restlessly round a glass bowl. A parrot sat
humped on his perch, gazing bleakly into space.

There was a notice in the window: PUPPIES FOR
SALE. Magnus could see them at the back of the shop,
curled up in a round wicker basket. There were half a
dozen of them, all mixed up together, homeless waifs
awaiting their fate.

'Can I help you, sonny?'

Magnus had never been called sonny before, and did
not like the sound of it. He glared up at the man who
had spoken, and saw a bright-red face and a pair of
shaggy eyebrows glistening with drops of rain. His eyes
had a kind look in them, and Magnus forgot his anger
when he realized who the man was.

'Mr Archie Tosh!'

'That's right.' The eyebrows shot up and down, and
drips of rain fell from them on to the man's red cheeks.
'What can I do for you?'

'It's the dog,' said Magnus, pointing to Rory sitting
patiently on the wet pavement. 'He's going blind.'

'Is that so? Come in, sonny, and we'll see what can
be done about it.'

Half an hour later Magnus came out alone. It had

not been easy leaving the dog behind. Rory looked up at him with dazed eyes and gave a pathetic whimper. 'Don't leave me,' he seemed to be begging.

'It's all right, Rory. Mr Tosh'll look after you,' said Magnus in a shaky voice.

'He'll soon settle down,' said the vet confidently. 'You take yourself off, sonny.'

Magnus felt that he was parting from his last link with Sula. From now on he was alone amongst strangers. There was not a familiar sight to be seen. No Heathery Hill. No peat-stacks. No Gran clumping about in her big boots.

It was still raining. Little rivulets trickled down the gutters, and the people were huddled in doorways like wet hens. Magnus felt suddenly deflated, as if all the stuffing had been knocked out of him. His damp suit seemed tighter. His feet hurt in his Sunday boots, and the lump in his throat had grown bigger.

He walked round the corner and found himself in a quieter street. Cairn Terrace, it was called. There were no shops here, only rows of houses with names on the gates. He walked past The Sheiling, Grey Gables and The Knowe, searching for Rockview. He found it near the middle of the terrace.

Magnus paused before opening the gate. It was a real gate leading into a garden path. In Sula a gate could be anything, from an old bedstead to a piece of wire-netting tied up with binder-twine. Here, everything was prim and neat. Even the flowers stood to attention in rows, and there were no weeds, nettles, or thistles to be seen.

Every door in town, unlike those in Sula, was firmly

shut. Magnus wondered if he should turn the handle of Rockview and walk in, or if he should knock. Then he saw the bell. How did it work, he wondered? He hesitated, then pressed his finger on the little knob and jumped back in surprise when he heard a jingle-jangle from inside. He would have darted away if the door had not suddenly opened.

'Hullo. Is it yourself, Magnus Macduff?'

'Uh-huh! It's me.'

The woman who had opened the door – Mrs Reekie – had a faint look of old Cowan about her. Somehow it made the boy feel less lost and homesick. It was some contact with Sula, however remote.

Mrs Reekie was small and stout, like a plump little hen. Her reddish hair wound round her head in plaits, and she was encased in an overall with a design of vivid flowers – purple poppies mixed up with yellow roses and blue leaves. Magnus stared at it, thinking the man who designed it must have gone mad with his paint-box. He longed to tone it down and put in some subtler shading.

A child stood behind Mrs Reekie, clutching at her skirt, a small red-haired replica of her mother. She took little peeks at Magnus now and again, then sat down with a bump on the linoleum and stayed there sucking her thumb.

Mrs Reekie opened the door wider and gave Magnus a friendly smile. 'Come away in. I was just saying to Willy Reekie, I wonder where Magnus Macduff is. The boat's been in for ages. I thought maybe you'd got lost. In all this rain, too. I was just saying to Willy Reekie the laddie won't think much of Cronan.'

Mrs Reekie was always 'just saying' something. It was a record that went on and on. Magnus wondered how anyone could find enough words? He could not take it all in. A short sentence was as much as he ever spoke in Sula.

'And how's everybody?' she asked, as he followed her along the passage-way.

'Fine,' said Magnus. Full stop.

Mrs Reekie could have done better. She could have made a long story out of Jinty's pimples. Or she could have told about old Cowan's goat butting the minister in the hindquarters. Or about the fishing being only so-so, and that they had taken the black-faced sheep to graze on Little Sula. She could even have found something to say about Gran's aspidistra.

She waited to hear if he had anything to add, but as nothing was forthcoming, she hoisted up the child and told Magnus, 'Her name's Ailsa. We call her our wee afterthought! We've got a grown-up son. Fancy that! Married and away living in Glasgow. So Ailsa's our wee ewe-lamb. Come on in, Magnus, and meet my husband. Are you there, Willy Reekie? Here's Magnus Macduff.'

Chapter 4

THE DUKE'S CASTLE

Magnus woke bright and early next morning. He was about to leap out of bed to take his first look at Little Sula, as he always did at home. He could tell what the weather would be like by the way the small island stood out in the sea, or faded into the mist.

Then he remembered. He was not at home. He was in a cramped little room, all rosy wallpaper, pink eiderdown, and floral carpet which had surely been designed by the man who had splashed the flowers on Mrs Reekie's overall.

It was like being in prison. He lay looking at the ceiling, the only white surface he could see, drawing mental pictures on it of moles and hedgehogs and seals. He was longing to get up, yet not wanting the day to begin. It held nothing for him but emptiness.

Suddenly the door was pushed open. The child Ailsa – the wee afterthought – stood staring at him with un-

blinking eyes. Then she tottered forward on her un-
steady legs and dumped something on the bed. It was a
small kitten, all fluff, like a soft toy.

'Goo! Foo! Oof!'

Ailsa had a language of her own. She was going to be
a talker like her mother, but as yet she had no real
words.

Magnus sat up in bed and patted the kitten. The
heavy feeling at his heart grew lighter. 'It's nice,' he
said, watching it closely. Like a small tiger. He would
draw a picture of it as soon as he had the chance.

'Oof-foof!' agreed the child.

Just then Mrs Reekie poked her head round the open
door. She was wearing a different overall this morning,
all yellow-and-black stripes, like a wasp.

'Would you care for a cup of tea, Magnus?'

'What?' he said in alarm. 'In bed? No thanks, Mrs
Reekie. I'll get up.'

'Right! The bathroom's free. They're all at their
breakfasts.'

'They' were Mrs Reekie's boarders. They came and
went. Some were regulars who returned year in, year
out. Others were commercial travellers who carried
samples and wrote up their orders in the parlour at
night.

Magnus need not bother with them. He was to live
with the family and have his meals in what Mrs Reekie
called the living-room-kitchen. It was at the back of the
house, looking out on a strip of garden with the harbour
beyond. And beyond that lay Sula, unseen, far away in
the distance.

Magnus had met the family the night before. Willy

Reekie sat in his shirt-sleeves, dandling the after-thought on his knee and singing 'Tooral-ooral-ooral-ay'. He was small and as wiry as a terrier. He had a rumpled face which broke into a comical grin when he was amused; and he had a deaf ear which turned towards his wife when she scolded him.

'Willy Reekie, put on your jacket. D'you hear me? Where's your manners? Willy Reekie! What'll Magnus think of you?'

The other member of the family was Auntie Jessie. She was a stout comfortable woman with bad legs. 'Varicose veins,' she told Magnus in case he had not noticed. 'I've had them all my days. I have to wear elastic stockings. They help a bit, but I've got to put my feet up whenever I can.'

There was a special footstool for her. Auntie Jessie's footstool. It added to the clutter in the already crowded room. Magnus, used to the bareness of Gran's cottage, had never seen so many things in the one room before: chairs, tables, sofas, pot-plants and ornaments.

The walls were covered with pictures: scenes of Cronan Bay and Highland cattle and the Queen with a crown on her head. On the mantelpiece there were china dogs and ducks and 'presents from Rothesay'. There was also a photograph of a plain young man with a self-conscious smile on his face.

'Our Andy,' said Mrs Reekie proudly. 'Away in Glasgow.' She gave a sigh as if Glasgow was the end of the earth.

Magnus was amazed at the way they were always talk-talk-talking. He and Gran scarcely exchanged a dozen words a day. But here they never stopped. Especially Mrs Reekie and Auntie Jessie. He had seen a couple of gannets doing much the same thing, stretching out their necks, each trying to get their word in first.

The Reekies talked about everything and anything. It was as if they were afraid of silence. When Magnus went down for his breakfast in the morning they were still at it, as if they had never stopped. They broke off when he came in, and said, 'Good-morning,' then waited for him to answer back. Gran would have given him a glance, if that.

'Hullo,' he said, uneasily, and sat down at the table.

'Willy Reekie's away to his work,' said Mrs Reekie, laying things on the table. 'D'you like your eggs hard or soft?'

'Anyway,' said Magnus, surprised to be getting an egg at all, and it not Sunday. Every day seemed to be a feast day at the Reekies'. Toast and marmalade. Wee curly pats of butter. Morning rolls, which Mrs Reekie called *baps*.

'Eat up!' She placed a boiled egg in a china egg-cup – a present from Dunoon – and laid a little horn spoon beside it. 'You'll be going out to see the sights?'

'What sights?' asked Magnus, looking up in surprise.

'Mercy me!' cried Auntie Jessie, amazed at his lack of enthusiasm. 'The town, of course. It'll be a treat for you after living on that desert island. Nothing but peat-reek and seagulls. How you can stand it beats me. Are you never fed up?'

'No,' said Magnus. But it was not true. He was fed up right now.

'Were you ever there, Jessie?' asked Mrs Reekie, for the sake of talking. 'In Sula?'

'Not me. I don't fancy it. Were you?'

'Yes, once. When I was a lassie. Years before I met Willy Reekie. I had just started work at the castle. Och, I've told you all about it before, Jessie. You remember, I went across to visit my cousins, the Cowans.'

'Och yes, so you did.' Auntie Jessie put her bad legs up on the footstool. 'How did you get on?'

'Get on! My! was I glad to get back to civilization! Wait till I tell you . . .'

They were off again on one of their endless dialogues. Magnus switched off, and thought his own quiet thoughts. Now and again their voices came through to him. They were talking of Cronan Castle and the Duke. It was a favourite topic of theirs, life in the castle when they had both worked below stairs.

Presently Auntie Jessie got up with a groan and said, 'This'll not mend the bairn's breeks! They'll have finished their breakfasts by now. I'll away and clear the tables.'

'And I'd better go and make the beds. Come on, Ailsa,' said Mrs Reekie, taking the wee afterthought by the hand.

The child toddled off with her mother, and Magnus was left to his own devices. Feeling stifled in the house, he went out and hurried down the garden path. He opened and shut the neat little gate, then turned his steps towards the harbour.

The *Hebridean* was still there with no one on board except a solitary seagull sitting on the funnel. A wild thought came into the boy's head. What if he were to start up the engines and sail back to Sula on his own? He knew it was hopeless, but even the thought of it gave a lift to his spirits.

He climbed on to the harbour wall and looked out across the water, wondering what Gran would be doing. He never thought about her when he was at home, but now he kept seeing her in his mind's eye. Was she emptying the teapot out of the door, drenching Specky the hen with tea-leaves? She might be milking the cow, gutting fish, gathering driftwood, cutting peat, or mending a drystone dyke. Anything except sitting still with her hands folded, or gossipping like Mrs Reekie and Auntie Jessie.

Gran and Old Whiskers were the two he missed most. What could he find here to take their place? He jumped off the wall and wandered up to the High Street. At the corner he stood and stared at the restless traffic and at the crowds. Where in the world were they all going in such a hurry? They were like the mice on the treadmill.

For the first time in his life Magnus was at a loose end. At home the days were never long enough. He could have been climbing the Heathery Hill. He could have been helping Gran in a hundred ways on the croft. He could have been rowing across to Little Sula, or lying on the rock beside Old Whiskers. But what could he do here in the midst of all this noise and confusion? He could not even get peace to think.

'Get out of the way, you!'

A violent push sent Magnus staggering off the pavement, almost in the teeth of a bus which was roaring up the High Street. He whipped round and raised his fists. He could have done with a fight to cheer himself up, if only the Ferret had been here. But the boy who had pushed him was running off, followed by half a dozen more, all as alike as peas in a pod. Neat shorts, navy-blue blazers, school badges.

A gaggle of girls in the same navy-blue came along, swinging their school-bags, all chewing and chattering. Magnus watched them making their way towards the gates of a rambling building at the top of the street. The High School; that was it! The place where he was to go to collect his prize. Maybe! He was not sure that he wanted it enough.

It looked too much like another prison, a treadmill where the mice were all dressed in navy-blue. Magnus turned away and went back to the pet shop, the only familiar sight he knew. He was staring in at the window when he heard a buzzing sound beside him. A tattered little man was also looking in at the prisoners, humming to himself like the Ferret buzzing in the schoolroom. Sometimes he swiped the air as if hitting out at an imaginary enemy. Sometimes he laughed or gave a shout. He seemed to be living in another world, but it was a cheerful world, wherever it was.

He looked at Magnus and grinned. 'Hullo, boy,' he said and gave Magnus a wink.

'H-Hullo,' said Magnus cautiously. He hoped the man was not going to be another talker. But he need not have worried. The little man had said his say, and now relapsed into silence.

The two stood side by side gazing in at the captive animals. Suddenly the little man wrinkled up his face and asked Magnus, 'Do you ever feel like breaking a window?'

Magnus nodded. His heart warmed towards the little man. They both shared the same feelings.

'Good! You're all right,' said the man, doing a kind of step-dance on the pavement; but that was as far as the window-breaking went. Magnus took a closer look at him and saw that he was dressed in ancient plus-fours, with down-at-heel boots, and leather patches on the elbows of his jacket. An old deer-stalker hat was perched on his head. He might have been any age from fifty to eighty. His face was criss-crossed with wrinkles, but his eyes were bright blue and lively. They seemed to be seeing things that were not there.

Who was he? A tramp? Or a gamekeeper, maybe?

'D'you like animals?' the man asked, nodding towards the pet shop window.

'Uh-huh!' said Magnus, in a decided voice.

'Me, too,' cried the little man. 'Which do you like best? Cats? Dogs? Horses? Weasels? Foxes?'

'Seals,' said Magnus.

'Good for you!' The little man did another step-dance on the pavement. 'Where do you come from, boy?'

'Sula.'

The little man threw his hat in the air and caught it neatly as it came down. He dumped it back on his head and seized Magnus by the hand. 'Sula! That's the place! Though I haven't been there for years. Years and years and years.' He made a kind of tune out of it, as if it was a song. 'I must go back again soon. Can you walk, boy?'

What a question to ask Magnus! 'Yes, of course, I can walk.'

'Come on, then. Follow me. Come home and talk about Sula. Years and years and years. . .'

For a time they walked together in silence, and yet not together. They had to separate to let people push past them. The little man took no notice of anybody. Sometimes he burst out laughing. Sometimes he gazed up into the sky. Now and again he took a little trot forward. It was almost like being with Rory in the days when the dog was younger and friskier.

They went up past the High School, past rows of bungalows on the outskirts of the town, out into the main road. They had to scurry on to the grass at the side to avoid the cars, buses, and lorries which came and went in a never-ending convoy. They were all trying to get past each other, as if it mattered that they saved a fraction of a second. Why were they all in such a frantic hurry, Magnus wondered?

Suddenly the little man turned in at a gate. It was no ordinary gate. This was a massive iron structure with strange designs on it – animals, fishes, shields. Worked into the pattern were the words CRONAN CASTLE. A forbidding notice was posted up: PRIVATE. KEEP OUT.

As the gate clanged behind them Magnus looked around him uneasily. He seemed to be in a wilderness of weeds, nettles, long grass, overgrown shrubs and bushes. The driveway was pitted with ruts and covered with moss. It went winding up towards the biggest building he had ever seen. Cronan Castle.

'Where are you going?' he called out to the little

man who was walking ahead, swiping at the nettles.

'Home,' said the man, pointing to the great castle.

'Mercy me!' Magnus stood stock-still. The truth was dawning on him. The tattered little tattie-bogle must be the owner of the castle. 'Are you him? The Duke?'

'Yes, that's me. Come on, boy. Don't dawdle.'

Magnus walked on in a daze. As the towers and turrets of the crumbling castle came nearer, he heard an eerie screech. A great bird was stepping in a lordly manner across the untidy lawn. It preened out its tail feathers into a spray of colours, the like of which Magnus had never set eyes on. What a picture it would make! He could have stood and watched it all day.

There were other creatures roaming about: dogs, donkeys, ponies, a tame fox sitting on its tail, a deer rubbing its horns against a tree-trunk, an old owl sitting hunch-backed on a post.

A gardener, like Old Father Time, was wielding a scythe in the undergrowth. He touched his cap to the Duke, who took no notice of him but hurried up the steps and vanished into the castle, followed by a scurry of barking dogs. Magnus followed, too, in time to see the little man pull off his shabby hat and fling it across the great hall, where it landed neatly on a stag's horn.

There were heads and horns, swords and shields, all around the walls. There was a fireplace big enough to roast an ox, and a great stairway wide enough for a coach-and-pair. The dogs went scampering up, followed by the Duke, who called out, 'Come on, boy. Up to the Tower.'

Magnus had never climbed so many stairs before. In

Gran's cottage nine steps led up to his little bedroom.
Here, one floor led to another and another and another;
and finally up a winding stairway to the tower.

It was obviously the Duke's sanctuary, filled with a
clutter of schoolboy treasures – cricket bats, stamp col-
lections, birds' eggs, bows-and-arrows, a telescope, a
model railway, a fiddle, books, music, photograph al-
bums, and piles of old newspapers.

'I never read them,' said the Duke, pushing them
aside to clear a space on the sagging sofa. 'Sit down,
boy.' But the dogs had already leapt up and taken
possession. Magnus sat down on the floor instead, with
the little man perched beside him on a footstool, like a
gnome on a toadstool.

The Duke took up a magnifying glass and rum-
maged through the pages of an old photo album.
'There! Do you recognize it?'

It was Sula. In the faded picture Magnus could see
the houses at the harbour, the school with the Heathery
Hill in the background, and a young man in a kilt standing outside the Cowans' door.

'That's me,' said the Duke, peering through the magnifying glass. 'Years and years ago. Years and years and
years. Tell me about Sula, boy.'

Normally, this would have been enough to make
Magnus close up like a clam. Words were never easy to
find. But there was something about the Duke – the
same something that drew him to Old Whiskers –
which made the boy feel at ease. Suddenly he found
himself speaking. Telling about Sula seemed to bring
the island nearer.

It came out in a spate, all the bottled feelings which

had been corked inside Magnus for years. He fixed his eyes on the window, with its faraway view of the open sea, and told of his life in Sula, his longing for solitude, his desire to do nothing but draw pictures of the wild life on the island. He spoke of Gran, of the school-master, of Mr Skinnymalink, and – more than anything – of the seals. Finally, he told his reason for coming to Cronan, and why he had to wait – an unwilling exile – till he could take Rory home.

Anyone who knew Magnus would have been astounded. He was astounded himself at his flow of words, and came to a sudden standstill. He took a look at the little man who was nodding and smiling and clapping his hands.

'How long before you can take the dog home?' asked the Duke.

'I don't know. A week or two, maybe.'

A week or two of listening to Mrs Reekie and Auntie Jessie talking about nothing, of wandering aimlessly about the streets, and never seeing a glimpse of Old Whiskers.

The little man had jumped to his feet and was talking to himself. 'Yes, that's it! I'll do it! Why not? Nothing to stop me. I'll take the dog back to Sula. It's years and years and years . . .'

It seemed years before Magnus could take in the full meaning of the Duke's words. Did it mean that *he* would be free to return to Sula as soon as the *Hebridean* sailed? The little man would look after Rory and bring him back as soon as he was well enough to travel. It was such a wonderful reprieve that Magnus did not know what to say.

'That's great!' he cried, wanting to clutch the Duke's hand and thank him properly. But now that he needed the right words, he could not find them. In any case, the subject seemed closed, as far as the Duke was concerned.

He had picked up the old fiddle and was tuning the strings. Then he sat down on the stool and began to play. The dogs buried their heads between their paws, and Magnus stared out of the window letting the music lap over him like the waves of the sea.

He was listening and yet not listening. He could hear the cry of the gulls, the moaning of the wind, the restless rustle of the leaves, and the waves splashing against the rocks. The music tugged at the boy's heart, making him more than ever homesick for Sula.

Surely the fiddle was telling a story. It was as plain to see as a picture. Magnus had a vision of the white horses on the water, the seals drifting on the surface, the blackcurrant bushes bending in the breeze, the Northern Lights – the Merry Dancers – flaring across the night sky. It was Sula as he knew and loved it.

A last ripple of notes, like the dipping of oars in calm water, and the music died away. Sula faded from sight, and Magnus shook himself awake from his half-dream.

'Did you like that, boy?' asked the Duke, laying down his fiddle. 'I played it specially for you. I call it my Sula Symphony. I wrote it years ago after visiting the island. Years and years ago. I should have it here somewhere.'

He hunted through an untidy heap of music. Magnus was surprised to see pages and pages of ruled paper covered with squiggly marks, like small pictures. They were not words, nor were they drawings. They were symbols which the Duke seemed to understand and could translate into melodies.

Magnus looked at him with new respect, more drawn towards him than ever. It must be wonderful to hear musical sounds inside his head and write them down so that anyone could play them. And yet not anyone! The Duke hid his music away in a dusty corner as he – Magnus – kept his drawings to himself.

'It was great. I could see Sula,' said the boy, wanting to let the Duke know that he understood.

The little man beamed with pleasure. For years (years and years, as he would have said) he had kept his music a secret. It was enough to compose it and play it in his lonely tower. Till now he had felt no desire to share it. But the boy, with his talk of Sula, and his own secret passion, had awakened in the Duke a desire to communicate. Not with everyone, or anyone; only with the boy. A strong bond of friendship was being forged between them.

There was a step on the stair, a knock at the door, and an old woman in a white apron put her head round and said crossly, 'Your dinner's ready, Your Grace. Are you coming down?'

'In a minute, Bella. Off you go,' said the little man, dismissing her. He turned to Magnus. 'D'you want some food, boy?'

'No, thanks,' said Magnus. He wanted to get away on his own to think. The Duke understood and did not try to detain him.

They went down the stairway together. Magnus had glimpses of great rooms filled with old furniture and family portraits. The whole of Sula could have lived here. It seemed fit for giants rather than one small creature like the Duke.

They parted on the doorstep, no words needed. Magnus walked down the drive, past the preening peacocks, back to the town. The street-lights were switched on, a sight he had never seen before. They softened the harshness of the houses, but he would sooner have been at home watching the Merry Dancers.

Chapter 5

MAGNUS AT SCHOOL

On his first morning back on the island Magnus was out bright and early, leaping around like old Cowan's goat. He was tingling all over with the joy of living. He would have liked to shout out loud to let everyone know how happy he was to be home. But it was not in his nature. He had to keep even his happiness to himself.

Everything he saw pleased his eye, even the Ferret playing one of his daft games, holding his breath till he was red in the face and then exploding like a gun going off. Jinty was skipping outside her door to the tune of 'One-two-three-a-learie'. Tair was chuckling at Specky the hen who was zig-zagging about in a drunken fashion. She had been pecking at some rotten potatoes which had grown fermented. They were as potent as strong drink.

Jinty came skipping after him, trying to attract his attention. 'Would you like a shot, Magnus?' she asked, offering him her rope. It was a generous gesture, for

everyone on Sula had few enough possessions and
guarded them fiercely. All the same, Jinty knew it was
a silly thing to do. Like as not, Magnus would not
bother to answer. But, to her surprise, he went to the
length of shaking his head. It was always something.

He went off on his own round the back of the
Heathery Hill, past the silent tent where the tourists
were still sleeping. He was making for the Hermit's hut.
Mr Skinnymalink sometimes spent the night in the
schoolhouse with his nephew, Andrew Murray, but
more often he preferred the solitude of his own company.

He was sitting – a lean and gaunt figure – outside the
door, patiently polishing a stone. It was one of the small
coloured stones which could be found on the Heathery
Hill and across on Little Sula. The Hermit had a heap
of them hoarded inside his hut. He would polish them
for hours to bring out their colours.

Magnus stood silently watching him. Mr Skinnymalink knew he was there, but there was no need for
good-mornings or hullos. Mrs Reekie and Auntie Jessie
would have spoken a spate of words by now.

At length Magnus broke the silence. Pointing to the
stones, he said, 'I saw some of them in Cronan.'

They were in a jeweller's window – the Stones of
Sula – made into bracelets and brooches and rings,
every single one collected and polished by Mr Skinnymalink. Andrew Murray had sent them across to
Cronan in the hope of starting an island industry. But
the Hermit was not interested in the finished product,
only in the stones themselves.

A whistled tune came floating across the air. It was

an unfamiliar melody which caused Mr Skinnymalink to raise his head and listen. He caught sight of a red and a blue tammy. The tourists were up and stirring, building a fire outside their tent.

The Hermit scuttled back into his hut like a startled rabbit and closed the door. Magnus knew there was no use waiting. He turned to walk back towards the harbour, passing the tourists who waved to him, recognizing the boy they had seen on board the *Hebridean*.

'Hullo!' called out the one in the red tammy. 'Please to tell us where we can buy the tobacco.'

'There,' said Magnus, pointing ahead to the houses at the harbour. The Cowans' shop, which was the post office and general store, sold everything from pencils to pails. It was a bit different from the supermarket at Cronan, but Magnus liked it better.

'Thank you, please!'

The two men bowed to him as he went past. They were a polite pair, not likely to upset the peace of the island. Unlike some of the summer visitors who took possession of the place, leaving trails of debris in their wake. Tin cans, cereal packets, empty bottles.

They looked upon the islanders as 'natives', and tried to take photos of Gran as she went about her work so that they could show their slides when they got back home to civilization.

'Look! Isn't she quaint? One of the islanders cutting peat. That's the stuff they burn on their fires, you know. We couldn't get her to pose properly. That's why the picture's a little out of focus.'

There would be none of that with the Scandinavians, who seemed used to fitting into any background without making a fuss. All the same, Magnus did not like strangers in Sula. He preferred everything to be the same yesterday, today and for ever.

Like Old Cowan. Magnus found him standing staring at his sheep. Now and then he poked at one of them with his crook. It was a long-handled stick with a curved handle. Old Cowan had made it himself, cutting the wood, then paring and sand-papering the stem, before finally fixing on the head made from a sheep's horn. He used it in a dozen different ways, to catch a stray sheep round the neck, or drag one out of a ditch, to swipe at thistles and nettles, to dig down into the peat-stack, to lever himself over a dyke. It was as good as a third hand.

But he still needed his dog. 'What about Rory, then?' he called out to Magnus.

Magnus scuffled his feet and said, 'The vet thinks he'll be okay.'

'That's fine,' said old Cowan, leaning on his crook. 'When's he coming back?'

'Soon.'

'Who's bringing him? Are you going back?'

Magnus shook his head. There would be no going back to thon big town if *he* could help it. 'A wee man's going to fetch him,' he told old Cowan.

'What wee man?'

Magnus looked at him and came out with it, plain and straight. 'He's a Duke.'

'What?' cried old Cowan, leaning so heavily on his crook that he almost fell over. 'You don't mean the Duke from Cronan Castle?'

'Uh-huh!'

'Mercy goodness me!' Old Cowan was flabbergasted beyond words. His Adam's apple shot up and down, and he gulped, 'The Duke coming here! Goodness gracious me! We'll need to tidy the place up.'

'What for?' said Magnus, thinking of the crumbling castle and the wilderness surrounding it. 'He'll never notice.'

But old Cowan had caught sight of the minister coming out of his garden gate, and was off to tell him the news. Once the Reverend Morrison knew, it would spread round the place like a forest fire; but at least it would save Magnus from telling anybody else.

The school bell began to play its tinny tune. Jinty and the others trooped up from the harbour, but Magnus hung back. This was his first morning home, his first day of freedom. Why spend it cooped up in a musty schoolroom, like a mouse on a treadmill, when he could have the whole of Sula for a playground? He would do what he wanted for one day.

Besides, the teacher would be asking him questions. 'How did you get on at Cronan? Did you go to the High School? What did the Art Master say? Did you get the paint-box? What did you do about Gran's letter? What happened to Rory?'

'No! I'm not going!' he told himself, and dismissed the idea of lessons from his mind. He would go and seek out the seal instead. Old Whiskers never asked any questions.

'Here, you, you're going the wrong way!' shouted the Ferret, as they met head-on.

'No, I'm not,' said Magnus, giving him a shove.

The Ferret put up his fists in a half-hearted way. He

knew there was no point in starting a full-blooded battle with the school-bell ringing. 'I'll get you later,' he growled, and shuffled past, sticking out his tongue as a parting gesture.

Magnus ignored him and ran down to the harbour, dodging past Jinty who was mincing her way up the path.

'Oh, Magnus, are you not coming?' she cried out, in a disappointed voice. She had been looking forward to sitting near her hero once more, and had spent ages putting her hair in ringlets for the occasion. She had got rid of her spots, and was all set to charm him, with a string of beads round her neck and a dab of scent behind her ears. She had a bag of mixed caramels in her pocket. But what was the use if Magnus was playing truant?

'I'm not coming,' was all he said, but in such a way that Jinty knew it was useless. Unless! A ray of hope brought a sparkle to her eyes.

'Wait, Magnus,' she called out in a voice full of guile. 'Did you hear about the big bird?'

Magnus half-turned. 'What big bird?' he asked gruffly.

Jinty knew she had him! The words came tumbling out in a torrent. 'There's something wrong with its wings. The teacher found it on the shore, half-dead, and he's keeping it in the school to see if it'll get better. I'm awful sorry for it. It would be a terrible pity if it died.' A craftier note crept into her voice. 'I was wondering if you could maybe come and have a look at it, Magnus. You might save its life. Couldn't you not, Magnus?' She almost over-did it, looking at him sideways with a beseeching glance. He would not come for her sake, she knew, but he might come because of the bird.

Being Magnus, he did not say yes or no straight out. 'I'll see,' he mumbled, but it was enough for Jinty. She went off to school with a smug look on her face, fingering her beads.

'That was clever of you, Jinty,' she told herself. 'You're not daft!'

When Magnus reached his favourite rock, the young seals were frisking in the water, but he did not take his usual notice of them. He could only think of the wounded bird. What could be wrong with it? Was its wing broken? Or its leg, maybe? It would be a pity, right enough, if it died.

Old Whiskers came weaving through the water, pushing the young ones out of his way. He wheezed and grunted as he eased himself up on to the rock. 'Hullo,' said Magnus, and settled down beside him.

It would be great to lie here all day at peace with the world. Later on he might fling off his clothes and join the young seals in the water. He often swam with them, twisting and turning, letting them rub their bodies against his. They accepted him as one of their own kind.

But he was not in the right mood today. Through half-closed eyes he watched the gulls gliding overhead, engaged in their endless aerobatics. They made him feel drowsy. He would have floated off to sleep, except for a niggling worry at the back of his mind. What about that other bird lying wounded in the schoolroom? Dying, perhaps, while he lay here not caring.

'It's no use, Whiskers. I'll have to go.'

The old seal gave a sleepy grunt. What was wrong with the boy? He was as restless as the young ones in the water. Could he not stay still?

'I'll come back,' promised Magnus, and ran off, taking a roundabout route to the school. He wanted to avoid Gran's eagle eye. If she saw him she would call out, 'Mag-nus, cut some peat. Mag-nus, feed the hens. Mag-nus, mend the gate. Mag-nus!'

He ran, half-doubled, hoping to be unseen, and almost bumped into the front wheels of the District Nurse's bicycle. She was in a cheerful mood, and rang her bell at him as if playing a tune.

'Look out, Magnus, or I'll have you on my books, too.'

Things were looking up on the island. The Ferret's mother had scalded her arm with a kettle of boiling water. Better still by far, Mrs McCallum – Tair's mother – would soon be giving birth to 'a wee stranger'.

It would be a great event. A new life on Sula, and she – the District Nurse – would help to bring it into the world. She had been making daily (sometimes twice-daily) visits to Mrs McCallum, who would otherwise have gone about her work without turning a hair. Instead, Mrs. Gillies did her best to turn her into an invalid.

'You'll have to rest more, Mrs McCallum. Put your feet up and take things easy. Are you sure you're drinking plenty of milk? Remember you've got another wee life to think about now. Wait a minute; I'd maybe better try your blood-pressure.'

Magnus leapt out of her way as she came charging

at him. She put on her
McCallum's doing fir
head still full of her
close watch in case
girl, I'm sure.'

But it was to be a wee boy, ac
andum had told him.

'You're to have a little brother.'

'Oh, am I?'

'Yes. With red hair, and a dimple in his chin.'

So that was that. Avizandum was seldom wrong.

Having delivered her bulletin about Mrs McCallum, the District Nurse now turned her attention to another news item.

'Is it true about the Duke?' she asked, scenting gossip.

'What about him?' said Magnus, though he knew fine.

'He's coming here, to Sula?'

'Uh-huh!'

'Mercy! Where in the world will he stay? We've got no castles here. We can't put him in a pig-sty. He's related to royalty. Though I've heard he's a queer wee man, for all that.'

She looked expectantly at Magnus hoping for a titbit, but he remained dumb. He had no desire to discuss the Duke with a gas-bag like Mrs. Gillies.

'Oh well, I'd better get on my way,' she sighed, giving up the struggle. She would get nothing more out of the boy. He was as close as a clam. 'You might give me a shove off, Magnus.'

She hopped on one foot like a hen before re-mount-

, while Magnus ran behind her, pushing
ntil she settled in the saddle and pedalled
he hurried off to school, hoping to slip in

s lucky. The children were out in the play-
, let loose for their morning break. Black Sandy
ed Sandy were playing leap-frog. Cuddy-loup-
dyke, they called it. Jinty was bouncing a burst ball
inst the school wall. She glanced at Magnus side-
ays, but had enough sense not to say anything.

The Ferret rushed up to him ready for a wrestling-
match. Magnus accepted the challenge and they
clutched each other round the waist in a deadly em-
brace. They had been on the ground half a dozen times
when the bell rang. Each gave the other a parting kick.
Most of their games ended like this, in an undecided
draw, to be continued later.

Magnus slipped into his seat, hoping the teacher
would not notice him. But Andrew Murray had seen
him all right. Only he, like Jinty, was learning sense.
Leave the boy alone; there was no use pushing him.
Subtler methods could be used.

Magnus took a quick look round the schoolroom.
Jinty knew what he was looking for.

'There it is!' she said in an important whisper, pointing to a waste-paper basket behind the blackboard. It
was a relic of old Miss Macfarlane's reign, made of
wicker with several spokes missing. Andrew Murray
had been meaning to replace it. It was one of a dozen
things he had never got round to doing, like ordering a
new globe of the world, and putting up new pictures
on the walls. There was only a torn map of Scotland

and a dusty picture of Little Bo-Peep with her sheep everlastingly trailing behind her.

He had tried to tackle the most pressing problems first. It was more important to get to grips with his pupils. The waste-paper basket could wait. It was seldom used, anyway. Except today. Inside sat a dejected bird, cowering with fright. Now and then it pecked at its wing-feathers, as if trying to work them free.

Magnus watched the bird, never taking his eyes off it, and Andrew Murray watched the boy.

'Would you like to come out and have a look at it, Magnus,' he suggested in an off-hand manner, not making it too pointed. 'Perhaps you could find out what's wrong.'

Magnus was out of his seat like a shot and down on his hunkers behind the blackboard.

He made soothing noises to the bird who looked up at him with bright unblinking eyes. It was a solan goose, its wings stained and clogged with oil. It must have drifted ashore, unable to fly and fend for itself. It was both hungry and exhausted, but Magnus could see a simple enough way of helping it.

'Soap and water,' he said, and looked up at the teacher.

'Right! Off you go. Take it into the schoolhouse and see what you can do.'

The man was human, after all. Magnus gave him a grateful look. He grabbed the wicker basket and went off next door, with the bird fluttering feebly in the cage.

Gran was there doing her daily cleaning, and making preparations for the teacher's meal. Herrings in oatmeal. She gave Magnus a sharp look but made no comment. She could see that he was here for a purpose, and let him get on with it. The kettle was boiling. Magnus poured some water into a basin, found a sponge and a bar of soap, and set to work. The bird squirmed under his grasp, but Magnus held firm, steadily soaping and sponging. It was a slow tedious task. Gran had put on her old cloth cap and left long before it was over.

The bird lay exhausted. Magnus found some crumbs of oatmeal and tried to entice it to eat.

'Come on, try a wee peck. You're starving.'

Over and over again he held out his hand, and at last the bird took a feeble peck. Then another and another.

'Good! You'll soon be okay.'

There was a note of satisfaction in Magnus's voice. Gently he dried the feathers with an old towel, and soon the bird was fluttering about the kitchen, trying its wings.

'Wait! I'll take you outside,' said Magnus, catching the bird and putting it back in the basket. He carried it down to the harbour and set it on the sand. For a time it sat there cowering, with its back humped up. Then it shook out its feathers and took a little run along the shore like an aeroplane revving up. The next moment it was in the air, flying into the wind. It wheeled and turned, then sailed away across the sky.

Magnus had another picture at his finger-tips, ready to draw. He might even paint it if he could capture the pastel colourings of the bird against the bright blue of the sky.

The thought of the paint-box brought back memories of that day in Cronan when he had gone to collect his prize. He was passing the prison gates – Cronan High School – on one of his aimless walks, when he remembered about John Craigie, the Art Master.

The pupils were all shut up in their classrooms, and the building looked so forbidding that he would have passed by had it not been for the janitor. Magnus had no idea who he was, a fierce-looking man dressed up like an admiral of the fleet.

'What are you wanting?' he asked gruffly, coming to the gates and rattling a bunch of keys.

'Nothing,' said Magnus, giving him a look.

The boy was about to turn away when a man came flapping across the playground, with a black gown floating from his shoulders. He had an untidy look about him, like a crumpled paper bag. His hair was tousled, his shoe-laces loose, and he was hunting through his pockets in a fevered fashion. He pulled out a squashed packet of cigarettes and called to the janitor, 'Hamish, can you give me a light?'

'Certainly, Mr Craigie. Hold on a moment.'

No need for the admiral of the fleet to hunt in his pockets. He knew exactly where to find a box of matches, without any fumbling. He handed them over and said, 'Here you are, Mr Craigie. You can keep them, if you like.'

'Thanks, Hamish. I've been dying for a smoke and a breath of fresh air. I felt I'd burst if I didn't escape from the classroom for a few minutes.'

He lit his cigarette and took great gulps at it, puffing out the smoke from his nostrils like a dragon. Then he caught sight of Magnus outside the railings and strolled up to him.

'Hullo,' he said, in a friendly voice.

Magnus was about to bolt like a startled rabbit when suddenly he decided to stay and stand his ground. The paint-box was within his grasp. So was Mr John Craigie.

'Are you the Art Master?' he gulped out.

'Yes, I am,' said the man, looking surprised. 'And who are you?'

'I come from Sula,' said Magnus, fumbling in his pocket and bringing out a letter. 'Here! It's from Mr Andrew Murray.'

The Art Master let out a puff of smoke and cried, 'You're not that boy, the one who won the prize? Magnus Something.'

'Macduff. Uh-huh! That's me.'

'My goodness, am I glad to see you!' John Craigie threw away his cigarette, half-smoked though it was and shouted, 'Open the gate, Hamish. Let him in.'

When the gate was open he gripped the boy's arm as if afraid Magnus would vanish from his sight, and marched him towards the main door of the school building.

'We'll go into the staff room. There's nobody there just now. I must have a quiet talk with you. Look! this is my lot!'

He paused on his way along the corridor to peer through the glass window at his pupils. They were painting a jug set up on a table with an orange and apple lying at its side. 'Still life,' said the Art Master. 'Keeps them quiet for a while. What do you think of the pictures?'

The walls were covered with paintings – no Little

Bo-Peep here – all done by John Craigie's pupils. Except one. It held pride of place and had a familiar look about it. It was Magnus's own scene of Sula with FIRST PRIZE printed underneath it.

'It's a masterpiece,' said John Craigie, showing Magnus into the stuffy staff room. He flung himself down in an untidy heap on one of the chairs. 'You've got a great gift, my lad. What are you going to do about it?'

'Nothing,' said Magnus. Except keep on drawing to his heart's content. He liked the man well enough, but had no wish to be locked up in his great jail. Still life was not for him.

'But, my dear chap, you're an artist. Not like that lot in the classroom. I've been longing for years to get my hands on someone like you. Not that I could improve your drawing, but at least I could give you some guidance on technique and on the use of colour.'

He could see that his words were falling on stony ground, and added impatiently, 'You can't hide your talent for ever, you know. Cream must rise to the top. Think what a wonderful career you could make for yourself.'

But Magnus was backing towards the door, as if trying to escape from a trap. 'I just came for the paint-box,' he said gruffly, 'but it doesn't matter.'

John Craigie ruffled his unruly hair. 'It's here,' he said and fetched the paint-box from the cupboard. He opened it out and began going over the names of the different colours, sensing that at last he was gaining the boy's interest. 'You see, Magnus, if you mix this with that, you'll get violet . . .'

Magnus was having his first art lesson whether he liked it or not. And now, back in Sula, his fingers were itching to make a splash of colour on his own drawing-book.

Chapter 6

ADVENTURE AT MIDNIGHT

He kept the paint-box hidden in his bedroom in the dark cupboard which Gran called 'the press'. Sometimes he stole upstairs and experimented with the rainbow colours. It was easy enough getting the vivid colours – bright blues and green and reds. It was the subtler shadings he was after, to match a bird's feather or a seal's whisker, or to capture the olive of a herring-gull's egg, splatched with brown. But the most difficult of all was keeping anything hidden for long in such a small community as Sula.

The moment inevitably came when Andrew Murray asked him the direct question.

'Did you go to the High School at Cronan and collect your prize?'

'Uh-huh!'

'How did you get on with Mr Craigie, the Art Master?'

'Fine!' Magnus pulled a letter from his pocket. 'Here! He's sent you a letter.'

'Thank you,' said Andrew mildly. He was learning to give and take where Magnus was concerned. He read a few phrases of the letter. It was just as he expected. John Craigie had not taken long to find out that Magnus was 'difficult'.

'As stubborn as a mule. Can't get anything out of him. No ambition. See if you can knock some sense into him. A genius. Must not be allowed to waste his talent.' And so on.

Andrew pushed the letter aside and asked another question.

'Have you used your paint-box yet, Magnus?'

'Uh-huh!' said Magnus, shuffling from one foot to the other.

'Perhaps you'll let me see what you've done,' Andrew ventured, none too hopefully.

'I'll see,' said Magnus, but he knew fine, and so did the teacher, that he would never show anyone what he had done.

'All right,' said Andrew, knowing he would get no further. 'Go back to your seat and get on with your work.' After all, the boy was only a pupil who had to be kept in his place.

After school Magnus ran down to the harbour hoping to lure Old Whiskers out of the water. There were white horses running on the surface of the sea, and the young seals were honking their horns as they tumbled

about amongst the waves. Old Whiskers was not to be
seen. Unless the sun was shining, he seldom showed
himself.

In any case, Gran was shouting, 'Mag-nus! Come
here!'

He went and helped her with her never-ending tasks.
The door of the old hen-coop was needing repair. Magnus nailed it up neatly, then brought in a fresh supply
of peat, before fetching the sheep down from the
Heathery Hill. He whistled tunelessly as he went about
his jobs, happily absorbed in what he was doing. Suddenly he thought of Mrs Reekie and Auntie Jessie in
Cronan saying, 'Are you never fed up on that desert
island?'

'Never!' he shouted to the startled sheep. How could
anyone be fed up on Sula, with such a variety of things
to do?

Gran finally sent him off with a can of milk for the
campers. He had meant to leave the milk-can outside
their tent and skedaddle away without having to speak
to them. But they were both standing outside the tent.
Magnus started in surprise when he saw what they
were doing. Painting a picture! There it was, set up on
an easel. The one in the red tammy was daubing at it
with his brush, while the other was standing by, looking on.

Magnus held his breath and longed to creep forward,
unseen, so that he could examine the picture at close
quarters. All he could see was a blur of blues and
purples and pinks, with an outline of what looked like
the Heathery Hill in the background.

The men were talking to each other in their own

language. They broke off when they saw the boy, and one of them said politely, 'Thank you, please,' as Magnus laid down the milk-can. 'Very kind.'

Magnus was about to dart away when the man with the paint-brush called, 'Wait!' He spoke quickly to his companion, addressing him as Sven.

'Ja!' Sven nodded his head and glanced at Magnus. 'Ja, that is a good idea, Bjorn. You stay, boy. We put you in the picture. Is good? You understand?'

Magnus understood only too well. They were wanting him to pose for them. He shook his head violently, and took to his heels, leaving them staring after him in surprise. What had they done to offend the boy?

Bitter memories of last summer when the film-makers invaded Sula flooded back to Magnus as he rushed away. He had been hounded by them and their cameras. Their inquisitive eyes had followed him every-where, peering and prying like private detectives. 'Human interest' was what they were after. Well, he was not going to provide it either for a camera or a paint-brush.

He remembered the day in Cronan when he had been walking along the High Street with the Duke. They had gone together to visit Rory at the vet's. The dog had his eyes bandaged and was lying still, pathetically quiet. But he roused himself to lick Magnus's hand, and responded to the Duke's kind voice when he spoke to him. Magnus felt relieved when he heard the little man's quiet words and saw how quickly he had gained Rory's confidence. It would be safe to leave him in charge of the dog's return home.

Archie Tosh, the vet, showed them out and left them

gazing in at the pet shop window. The Duke began to bubble with rage, like a kettle on the boil, as he watched the caged creatures turning round and round in their restricted space.

'I've a good mind to go in and punch that shopkeeper on the nose,' he cried, doubling his fists and thumping the air. He would have thumped the window as well, if Magnus had not caught his arm. He shared the Duke's anger, and liked him for it, but he knew it was wasted.

'Come on for a walk,' he said, as if talking to Rory; and, obedient as the collie, the little man followed him, still thumping the air with his fists.

It was raining again in a dismal downpour, wetter rain than in Sula. The cars splashed it up as they rushed past, so that the people on the pavement were drenched from below as well as from above. A flock of sheep came straggling across the High Street, up from the boats. They had come from one of the islands and were now being driven, poor things, to their doom. Before long they would be in the Glasgow shops, dead as mutton.

The downpour grew into a torrent. Everything looked dark and gloomy. Then suddenly a miracle happened. The street-lights were switched on by an invisible hand. Magnus gave a gasp. It was like a transformation scene. Gone were the dreary streets, replaced by pathways of shimmering lights, reflected in the wet roadway. It was as if the Merry Dancers had descended, shooting off scarlet and orange-coloured beams of brightness. Even the drenched people looked different, splashing through rainbow pools of light.

Magnus forgot the rain, seeing only the sudden
beauty of the scene. But the little Duke turned up his
collar and hunched his back like a wet stirk. Suddenly
he drew Magnus aside under a canopy for shelter. 'In
here, boy! Out of the rain!'

It was the local picture-house: THE GRAND
CINEMA. A man, grander than any cinema, was pac-
ing backwards and forwards in his fine uniform, all
polished buttons and gold braid. He looked as if he
owned the place, but gave a humble enough salute
when he saw the Duke.

'Good-evening, Your Grace; are you coming in?'

'What's on?' asked the Duke, shaking the rain from
his tattered garments. 'Anything worth seeing?'

'There's a documentary . . .' began the man; but
Magnus was not listening. He was staring at a blown-up
picture advertising the documentary, a picture of a
place so familiar that his heart almost stopped beating.

It was the harbour at home with the Heathery Hill
in the background, and some figures in the foreground.
Surely that was Gran bending down to pick up a load
of peat, and old Cowan mending his net. Another
picture showed sea-birds nesting on the crags, and a
rock where a boy lay side-by-side with a seal.

The words on the poster read: SUMMER IN
SULA: An Island Paradise.

'D'you see that, boy?' said the Duke in an excited
voice.

'Uh-huh!'

Magnus was still standing in a daze, gaping at the
pictures. He remembered the letter in his pocket, the
one addressed to Gran. It was an invitation from the

film-makers for him to attend the opening of the film and the reception afterwards as a 'guest of honour'. But he had not bothered about it.

Receptions were not for him, and he would sooner see Sula as it really was than through the eyes of a camera looking for local colour. All the same, his heart was thumping at the thought of seeing home, here in an alien town, even if it was only a blown-up copy of the real thing.

The little Duke was hunting through his pockets for money. He brought out a collection of odd coins and dumped them down at the pay-desk.

'Come on, boy,' he said, collecting the tickets and taking Magnus by the arm. 'Let's go in and have a look.'

They went, stumbling, into the dark interior of the cinema. An usherette with a torch led them to their seats. Magnus blinked his eyes, feeling like a mole. He could see nothing at first except vague figures all around him. Then his eyes focused on the screen in front.

The film had already begun. Magnus could hear pibroch music in the background and see a wide expanse of blue sea, with waves breaking in towards the shore. The music faded, and a man spoke in a voice that was too loud and too 'put on'. It might have been old Miss Macfarlane telling the story of the Three Bears. Magnus recognized it as the voice of the man, Jeremy, who had been directing the filming last summer.

'In this never-never land where time has stood still, the simple people set about their homely tasks untroubled by thoughts of the stirring world beyond their small horizon . . .' They were just words; they meant nothing to Magnus.

A ripple of music, then a close-up of some of the simple people : the District Nurse wheeling her bicycle and waving cheerfully, knowing that the camera was watching; the minister digging in his garden, wearing his dog-collar and smiling to nobody in particular; Tair standing on his head; the Ferret playing cuddyloup-the-dyke with Black Sandy and Red Sandy; glimpses of Gran carrying a pail, and of Jinty Cowan, with her hair in ringlets, posing outside her door, trying her best to look like a leading-lady.

Magnus sat bemused, watching it all and listening to the sickly sweet commentary. The man, Jeremy, and his camera had missed nothing. The school, the church, the pier, the boats, the Heathery Hill, Little Sula, even Specky the hen, and Bilko the goat, were all there. The boy squirmed in his seat when he saw himself – always a back view – running away from the camera, except for that furtive shot they had taken when he was lying asleep on the rock with Old Whiskers by his side.

'A scene of island bliss, far removed from the busy bustling world,' the commentator went on. 'The boy and the seal lie undisturbed . . .'

Undisturbed, Magnus thought bitterly, except for the camera's prying eye.

Everything in the cinema was too big and too hot and too loud. A woman sitting next to Magnus was munching crisps which crackled like gun-shots. 'Wheesht!' he wanted to say to her. The Duke did better. He leant across and hissed fiercely, 'Shut up, woman!'

Startled, she crumpled the paper bag in her lap and

stared at the screen in silence. But in a few moments her hand stole out, and the fumbling and crackling started all over again.

They were launching the life-boat in Sula, though the sea was as calm as a mill-pond. 'And in times of stress,' boomed out the commentator, making a meal of it, 'every islander puts his hand to the wheel . . .'

The little Duke got up abruptly and said, 'I can't stand that man's voice another second. Come on out.'

They pushed past the woman with the crisps, and went out to the accompaniment of a lament on the bag-pipes. In the foyer Magnus blinked his eyes, hardly knowing where he was; in Cronan with the lights dancing on the wet streets, or in Sula helping to launch the life-boat.

'Stupid fools!' said the Duke, hunching up his shoulders against the rain. 'No sensitivity.'

Magnus was not sure what sensitivity meant, but he knew that the Duke shared his feelings about the film. Seeing Sula through the eyes of someone who lived there and loved the island would have been wonderful. But a stranger giving a tourist's-eye view had some-how made a mockery of it. As for helping to provide 'human interest', Magnus cringed at the very thought of it.

Magnus felt the same about the tourists who wanted to paint him into their picture. Yet the glimpse he had seen of the painting had whetted his appetite and made his fingers tingle to experiment with his own paints and brushes.

That night he worked in his cramped bedroom till

the light failed. He was completely absorbed, though he knew that he had not the right materials. He needed a canvas, a palette knife, oil and turpentine. Yet he did his best with what he had, feeling a thrill of excitement every time he dipped his brush into a new colour.

He had no lack of subjects. There was enough material in his mind's eye to keep him going; and if he looked out of the window he could see the setting sun shining on the water like the glittering street-lights in Cronan. He watched for the Merry Dancers but they were not to be seen tonight.

The man, Jeremy, would have made much of the scene in his commentary. 'The water laps lazily towards the shore. The gulls settle down to sleep on the rocks. The lights in the cottage windows go out one by one, as the simple people prepare for their well-earned rest. Soon everyone in this island paradise will be sound asleep . . .'

Magnus himself was sound asleep when a handful of pebbles came rattling against his window-pane. He was up like a shot, pushing open the window and leaning out to see what was the matter. A furtive figure stood lurking in the shadows, beckoning on him to come down. It was Mr Skinnymalink, the Hermit.

Magnus did not hesitate. He knew something serious would have to happen before Mr Skinnymalink would take the risk of wakening him at dead of night. In a few moments he was into his clothes, ready for action. How to get down the creaky stairs without disturbing Gran was not so simple.

He did not know what the time was or whether the big aeroplane had passed over. Under cover of its throbbing engines he could have stolen down unnoticed. But perhaps it was too late, or too early. It would be safer to climb out of the window and shin his way down.

Mr Skinnymalink reached up to break his fall as he came scuffling down like a cat-burglar.

'What's up?' asked Magnus breathlessly.

The Hermit drew him away from the cottages, down over the shingly beach to the water's edge. He pointed with a skinny finger across to Little Sula and whispered, 'Watch!'

Magnus watched, but he could see nothing except the vague outline of the small island. It was so tiny that sometimes in stormy weather, the sea swept over it and swallowed it in one gulp. But in calm weather it provided a good grazing-ground for the Sulan sheep when they needed a change of diet. Gran's black-faced ewes were on the island right now. Only yesterday Magnus had helped to row them across.

'What are you looking for?' he asked, puzzled at Mr Skinnymalink's intense gaze. 'There's nothing there, except the sheep.'

No sooner had he spoken than a faint flickering light could be seen on the island. It flared up for a moment and then went out.

'There!' said the Hermit, satisfied that he had not been mistaken. 'That's what I've been seeing.'

'What is it?' asked Magnus, straining his eyes. 'Maybe it's just a Willy Wisp.'

But Mr Skinnymalink knew a will-o'-the-wisp when he saw one. 'There's somebody there,' he croaked in his rusty voice. 'Somebody's trying to signal. Look!

There it is again. We'll have to go across.'

Magnus did not question him. It was an adventure. If the Hermit was game to go, so was he. As quietly as they could, they untied Gran's boat, pushed it into the water and climbed on board.

They dipped their oars gently, looking back at the silent houses. They could hear nothing except some sleepy animal sounds – a grunt from old Cowan's pig, a cough from Gran's cow, the whirring of a night-fowl's wing. There was no conversation from the Hermit. Having said his say, he had relapsed once more into his customary silence. Magnus wondered if they were making their journey in vain. Was Willy Wisp leading them astray?

He peered down into the dark sea, thinking of Old Whiskers and the other seals. Were they asleep or secretly watching? His heart began to beat faster as they neared the shores of the little island. There was no knowing what they might find there; but all he could see were the black-faced sheep huddled together, chewing as if their lives depended on it. Did they never stop eating, night or day?

Magnus and the Hermit jumped out as the boat reached the shallows, and were dragging it up on to the pebbly beach when a sudden sound broke the silence. It was the barking of a dog.

'Mercy me!' gasped Magnus, as amazed as if he had seen a ghost. 'It's Rory!' Or maybe it was Rory's ghost-voice.

The collie came bounding towards him, scattering the sheep out of the way. He leapt up to lick the boy's face, wagging his tail in a frenzy and panting with delight at the reunion. He was real and solid enough; no ghost.

'Good dog, good dog,' said Magnus, patting the collie's rough coat. 'How on earth did you get here?' Surely he could not have swum all the way from Cronan.

'I brought him, of course,' said a familiar voice. A little man loomed up out of the darkness and grunted, 'Hullo, boy. It's me.'

It was the Duke.

It took ages for Magnus to piece the story together and make some sort of sense out of it. The little Duke's way of talking was never very straightforward at the best of times. He pranced from one foot to another and said, 'Did you see my signal? I had nothing but a box of matches. I kept striking them, one after the other, hoping someone might see. I didn't fancy spending the whole night here without shelter, so I hoped someone would come to the rescue. This is Little Sula, isn't it?'

'Yes,' said Magnus, still in a daze, 'but how . . . ?'

The little man had turned to the Hermit and was saying, 'I know who you are. Mr Skinnymalink! Magnus told me about you. I was hoping to meet you when I rowed to Sula.'

'Rowed!' Magnus stared at the Duke. 'Did you row all the way from Cronan?' he asked in amazement.

The little man jumped from one foot to another. Then he held out his hands to show that they were covered with blisters. 'I haven't rowed for years and years,' he said, with a boyish grin. 'I used to be a good enough oarsman. Years and years and years ago. So I thought I would have a shot at it. The dog was well enough to travel. He'll be all right, the vet says. So, instead of waiting for the *Hebridean*, I decided to have an adventure on my own . . .'

Up till now he had looked like a schoolboy enjoying a forbidden prank. But suddenly his shoulders drooped and he seemed old and ill and exhausted.

'The trouble was,' he confessed in a weary voice, 'I lost my oars in the darkness and just drifted about, hoping the tide might take me ashore. And so it did, but not to the right place.'

He suddenly slumped, and the Hermit caught him in his skinny arms. In moments of crisis, Mr Skinnymalink could come to the surface and take command of the situation.

'Come on, Magnus,' he said briskly. 'Let's carry him to the boat. We'd better take him over to Sula. He can stay in the schoolhouse. Andrew has plenty of room.'

The little Duke had crumpled with weariness. He made no protest when they picked him up and put him in the boat. Rory was already there, standing in the prow, wagging his tail.

They rowed back in the moonlight, a strange cargo. The Duke was sound asleep, muttering and mumbling in his dreams. Rory swayed with the boat, never taking his eyes off the shore as they drifted nearer to it. He seemed to sense that a familiar haven lay ahead.

'It's all right, Rory,' said Magnus, putting a soothing hand on the dog's quivering back. 'You're home.'

Chapter 7

LIFE AND DEATH

It was a day of life and death on Sula: the day the McCallum twins were born, the day old Cowan's pig was to die. It was as well it was Saturday – a holiday from school – with so much going on.

It was inevitable, the killing of the pig. It had been reared for that purpose, like the sheep Magnus had seen straggling up the wet High Street in Cronan. They would die on alien soil, but the pig was to be killed at home in old Cowan's shed – if that was any consolation.

Magnus had often helped to feed Grumphy with potato-peelings and other swill. He knew, of course, why the animal was being fattened. Yet when the time came he shied away from all signs of slaughter: the sharpening of the knives, the boiling of great pots of water for scalding the carcase, the knotting of the rope that was to hang up the dead beast from the rafters of the shed.

The Ferret, on the other hand, gloated at the prospect, and would not have missed a moment of the drama. Moreover, he was looking forward to his 'perk'. It was the bladder of the deceased pig, which could be blown up and used as a football.

Magnus, too, would kick it, once the awful feeling had worn off. He would even eat the spare-ribs, the pig's-puddings, and the succulent salt ham which would be shared around. Meantime, he wanted to take himself off from the scene of execution. He would go to the far side of the island to hide from the squealing of the pig. He would put his fingers in his ears and hear the surging of the waves instead.

Magnus had already come face-to-face with the executioner. They had both emerged from their doors at the same moment, and old Cowan had stared in surprise – not at Magnus – but at the dog sitting waiting on the doorstep.

'Goodness gracious me! How did you get here?' he cried, looking at Rory as if he had dropped down from the sky.

The dog could only answer by jumping up and wagging his tail. It was left to Magnus to explain the mystery. The boy was looking paler than usual, weary after his night's adventures.

'The Duke brought him,' he told old Cowan straight out.

'What?' The knives the man was holding almost fell from his grasp. 'The Duke? Never! Where's he staying? How did he come?'

'In a boat. He's at the schoolhouse,' said Magnus and took to his heels. The sight of the sharp knives was turning his stomach. How could he stay and talk to someone who was about to slit Grumphy's throat? He knew the deed had to be done and that old Cowan would make it as speedy and painless as possible. All the same, for the moment he thought of the man as a murderer.

He had to pass by the pig-sty. There was no way of avoiding it. Try as he would, he could not help catching a glimpse of Grumphy restlessly routing in his trough. Was it too late to save his life?

Ting-a-ling-a-ling-a-ling.

Never had the District Nurse rung her bell with such triumphant vigour. It was like the pealing of church bells to announce a happy event. There was a blissful look on her face as she called out, 'Twins! A wee boy and a wee girl. Both with red hair and dimples. All doing well. Isn't it great?'

'Great!' cried Magnus, meaning it. For a moment he forgot the doomed pig. Two new lives in Sula. It was great news, right enough.

The District Nurse beamed at him. Today she loved the whole world. 'They're going to call the wee girl after me. Fancy that!'

She rode away as if on wings, still ringing her bell though there was no one in the way. Magnus had no idea what her name was. She was just Mrs Gillies. Maybe it was Morag, or Fiona, or Isabel. Or just plain Jean. Trying to puzzle it out took his mind off the slaughter of the pig for a short time.

Tair came whizzing out of the McCallum's cottage as if his clothes were on fire. He was talking to Avizandum in an excited voice.

'You were right, Avizandum. I've got a wee brother,

and a wee sister as well. The District Nurse brought them on her bicycle. Come on, let's see the pig being killed.'

Magnus hurried away out of ear-shot, scrambling up the Heathery Hill and round to the cave where the Hermit sometimes took shelter. It was empty except for a small heap of Mr Skinnymalink's coloured stones. Magnus sat inside, his head buried in his hands, trying to think of the newly-born babies and not of the dying pig.

Now and again he glanced at the coloured stones glowing in the dark cave: amber, deep purple, leaf-green, rose-red. Some day he would put them in one of his pictures.

A sudden sound disturbed his thoughts. Was it the screech of a seagull swooping down from the cliffs, or the last agonizing cry of the pig? Magnus dug his fingers into his ears until he could hear nothing but a buzzing sound. But suddenly another noise broke through. He could hear someone sliding and slithering round the hillside towards the entrance of the cave.

It was the Duke.

'Hullo, boy,' he said, and flung himself down at the entrance of the cave, panting for breath. He mopped his brow and grinned at Magnus. 'I'm supposed to be in bed resting. That teacher chap has sent for the District Nurse to look at my blistered hands, but I dodged out behind his back.'

He looked like a schoolboy playing truant. The little man had made a quick recovery. He seemed to be suffering no ill-effects except for his blistered hands.

Magnus saw how raw and sore they looked, and suddenly sprang to his feet.

'Wait there. I'll be back,' he told the Duke and went slithering down to the shore. He came back carrying handfuls of the edible seaweed called carrageen moss. 'Wrap it round your hands and it'll take the sting out of them,' he told the Duke.

Magnus had used the seaweed many a time to soothe his own wounds, and knew how to doctor himself by rubbing docken-leaves on nettle-stings, and sucking thorns from his fingers. It was better than being fussed over by the District Nurse.

The little Duke sat rubbing the seaweed between his hands. Now and then he broke off a piece and chewed it, like one of Gran's sheep chewing its cud.

'It's years since I've tasted carrageen. Years and years and years.' He drew a contented breath and gazed out over the water. 'It's great to be here.' Suddenly he turned to Magnus. 'Come on, boy. Tell me everything.'

It was surprising how Magnus could untie his tongue in the Duke's presence. Talking to him was not like talking to any ordinary grown-up. There was something of himself in the strange little man.

'Cowan's pig's been killed,' he began, feeling less sorry about it now that the deed was done. 'And Mrs McCallum's had twins. A wee boy and a wee girl.'

Having got rid of the two major events of the day, he went on to tell about the bird he had set free and about the tourists and their paintings.

'And what about yours?' asked the Duke, giving him a keen look.

'Mine?' Magnus drew back into his shell. 'Och, fine!' was all he would say.

'Maybe you'll let me see some,' said the Duke, feeling his way.

'Maybe,' said Magnus, but the Duke could see that the boy wanted to change the subject. He looked thoughtful for a moment and then said, half to himself, 'I've got a plan in my head. Yes, indeed I have! But we'll talk about it later. Come on, boy. Let's go and look for the seals.'

Magnus led the way down towards his rock. The Duke slithered behind him with the seaweed still wrapped round his hands.

'Wheesht!' Magnus warned him, as they neared the spot. 'Sit on the rock and I'll see if Old Whiskers'll come out.'

There was no sign of him nor of any of the other seals. Had they sensed the presence of a stranger? Magnus felt in his pocket for the home-made whistle he sometimes tried to play. He was no musician. Up the scale and down again was all he could manage but usually it was enough to coax the old seal out of the water.

Today the notes sounded shakier than ever. Magnus felt self-conscious playing in front of the Duke, and him a real musician. Indeed, he had only played a few notes before the little man freed his fingers from the seaweed and said, 'Let me! It's years since I played a whistle. Years and years. All the same, I'd like to try.'

He thumped the whistle on his knee and began to play. First he blew his way up the scale and down again, as Magnus had done. Then suddenly the notes began to fly through the air like bird-song, full of trills and twitters, and then weaved themselves into a dancing-tune. Magnus could not believe his ears. How could his battered old whistle produce such magic melodies?

The little Duke was enjoying himself. He beamed with delight as his blistered fingers coaxed one tune after another from the old whistle. Then suddenly Magnus saw the sleek heads bobbing up in the water. He kept silent, not wanting to break the spell. Gently he nudged the Duke and pointed to the seals.

They seemed to be dancing to the music, a kind of ring-a-ring-of-roses with Old Whiskers in the middle of the circle. It was a sight that any film-maker would have given a lot to capture.

The Duke played softer music, trying to lure the seals to the shore. They came floating nearer, fascinated by the sound, raising their heads to listen. Some seemed to be singing. Even Old Whiskers was grunting as if trying to join in the chorus.

Suddenly the spell was broken. The seals dived below the surface and vanished in a ripple of water.

It was Jinty. Magnus could have killed her. Too late she saw the mistake she had made, and cried out, 'Oh, Magnus, I'm awful sorry.'

Attracted by the music – like the seals – she had come dancing across the shingle, showing off as usual. She wanted the little Duke to see her doing the Highland Fling. He would be pleased to see how she could kick up her heels and step it out in time to his tune. She was wearing her best blue velvet frock in honour of everything that was happening today – the birth of the twins, the killing of the pig, the visit of a titled gentleman who was related to the royal family. But it was all spoiled by Magnus looking at her like a thunder-cloud about to burst.

'See what you've done, you stupid girl!' cried the Duke in a fury. 'Go away! At once!'

'Yes, Your Lordship, Your Grace!' She bobbed a curtsey to him. At least the Duke had spoken to her. Maybe, in spite of his anger, he had taken a fancy to her.

'Who was that pretty little girl in the velvet frock? The one who danced so beautifully?'

He would invite her to his castle, and introduce her to royalty, and she would become a lady-in-waiting. The Duke might even adopt her and leave her a fortune in his will.

'To my dear adopted daughter, Lady Jinty, who brought such sweetness and light into my last days.'

Then she and Magnus would get married and live happily ever after in Cronan Castle.

Meantime, she had been successful in one thing. She had driven away the seals for good. The Duke made a half-hearted attempt to recapture the spell, but it was no use. He was too angry. His fingers fumbled over the notes, and at length he flung down the whistle and wrapped his hands once more in their seaweed bandage. Nothing would bring the seals back now.

In any case, there were other noises to distract them. The Ferret was kicking the blown-up bladder about and fighting off Black Sandy who was shouting for his share of it. Great signs of activity could be heard from old Cowan's shed.

'We might as well see what's going on,' said the

Duke, grunting like Old Whiskers as he eased himself up from the rock. 'Come on, boy.'

Magnus had lost his feeling of compassion for the pig. It was not Grumphy any more, only a carcase. Its reeking entrails had been taken out, and the men were scalding the body with boiling water, then scraping off the hairy outer skin. Soon it would be strung up, and later cut into spare-ribs, and into hams which would be kept hanging from cleeks in many a cottage ceiling. Everyone in Sula benefited from a pig-killing.

At first old Cowan and the others were embarrassed by the Duke's presence. But when they saw how shabbily he was dressed and that he put on no airs and graces, they accepted him as one of themselves. All except the Reverend Alexander Morrison who was greedily awaiting his share of the spoils.

'Welcome to the island. It's a great honour to have you here, Your Grace,' he said in a fulsome voice, as if Sula belonged to *him*. 'I hear you rowed all the way. What a feat! I must say I admire your stamina. You'll come and take tea with me in the Manse, I hope.'

The Duke was saved from answering by the arrival of the District Nurse.

'Your Grace! Your Grace! I've been chasing you all over the place. Let me have a look at your hands. It's high time they were bandaged.'

The little Duke grumbled, but Mrs Gillies was more than a match for him. There and then she whipped out a roll of bandages and a box of soothing ointment from her black bag, and seized him by the hands, seaweed and all.

'Tut-tut!' she said, peeling it off. 'I can do better than that. Stand still, Your Grace.'

She was being fully-stretched today, right enough, what with the twins, and now a patient with royal blood in his veins. 'There!' she said, giving the Duke back his bandaged hands. 'I'll have another look at them tomorrow. Watch yourself, Your Grace!'

She bobbed a curtsey – as Jinty had done – and went on her way, a ministering angel, under royal patronage.

The Duke's hands were now so well wrapped-up that they hung useless by his sides. He could do nothing with them.

'Silly woman!' he grunted, edging away from the minister to speak to Magnus. 'Come on, boy. Let's get away by ourselves for a walk. At least that woman hasn't bandaged my feet.'

Rory came bounding after them. The collie was in high spirits, rushing here and there smelling familiar scents, wagging his tail and barking with joy. Magnus could enter into the dog's feelings. It had been the same with him on his first day home.

He rubbed the dog's ears and said, 'Good old Rory! It's great to have you back.' Then he turned to the Duke and said, 'Thanks a lot, Duke.' It was not much of a speech, but the little man knew that he meant it.

'Nonsense! It's thanks to you and Rory that I'm here in Sula. I haven't enjoyed myself so much for years and years.'

The dog ran on ahead, barking at everything. He nosed round the tourists' tent. The two men, Sven and Bjorn, had gone to join the others watching the cutting-up of the pig's carcase. They had left their painting behind on the easel. Magnus's heart began to beat faster at the sight of it. Now was his chance to examine it at close quarters.

Someone was already there, standing staring at it. The Hermit! He turned and gave them a startled look, then relaxed when he saw who they were.

'Hi, Mr Skinnymalink,' called the Duke. 'The very man I want to see. Thank you for what you did last night. If it hadn't been for you, I'd still be stuck on Little Sula.'

The Hermit looked down at the ground and shuffled his feet. He was not used to words of praise. 'About your boat,' he muttered.

'It'll still be there, I expect,' said the Duke. 'Round the far side. I managed to pull it on to the shore, but I was too exhausted to tie it up.'

Magnus looked at Mr Skinnymalink, 'We could go across later and fetch it back.'

'Okay,' said the Hermit, and loped away to continue his solitary pursuits.

Magnus hurried forward to stare at the picture. It was half-finished, mostly sea and sky and Heathery Hill. He looked enviously at the cloudy grey of the sky, the reddish-brown of the bracken and the soft green of the grass. Would he ever learn the secrets of such subtle shadings?

'Not bad,' said the little Duke, peering at the picture. 'I might buy it myself for the castle. Though I'd sooner have one of yours. That reminds me, boy.' He tried to put his bandaged hand in his pocket. 'I've got something to show you. It's in my pocket-book. Help me to get it out.'

Magnus did as he was bid. He pulled out the pocket-book, then the little man squatted down on the grass and motioned Magnus to sit beside him.

For years afterwards – indeed all his life – Magnus was to remember every single sight and sound and smell connected with that strange moment. The heavy breathing of the collie lying at his feet. The feel of the leather pocket-book in his hand. The cry of a sea-mew. The shouts of the children playing near the scene of the pig-killing. All his senses seemed sharpened, so that everything was stamped on his mind for ever.

He little thought what a thunderbolt was to come when the Duke indicated a photograph in his pocket-book and said, 'Take that out, boy and have a look at it. It's for you to keep. Remember when you were at the castle and I showed you one that was taken when I visited Sula long ago?'

Magnus nodded, still not knowing what was to come. The photograph, he remembered was of the Duke as a young man, standing outside the Cowans' door, wearing a kilt.

Now he held another photograph in his hand. 'I came across it the other day when I was rummaging about in the tower,' the Duke told him. 'I took it myself with my old box camera on my very last visit to Sula. Take a look at it, boy, and see if you recognize anyone.'

There were three figures in the picture, standing stiff and straight against the harbour wall: a young man and a young woman, with Gran in the middle. Gran! Imagine her posing for her picture! She was wearing her ordinary working clothes, but her expression seemed softer than usual. There was a happy look in her eyes and the hint of a smile on her lips. Magnus wished she would look like that more often. Why was she so happy, he wondered, and who were the other two with her?

He looked at the young man first, and his heart almost stopped beating. Surely there was something familiar about his face and about the Harris tweed suit he was wearing. It was the same pattern as the one Magnus himself wore on Sundays, made down from his father's suit.

The boy's hands trembled so much that he could scarcely hold the photograph steady. The young man was looking straight at him with a steady, friendly gaze. He looked strong and dependable, as if he could face any dangers without flinching. His eyes seemed to have a message in them. 'Don't worry! All's well! I'm here!'

The young woman was smiling at him, a gentle sweet smile. She was pretty, with fair curls falling about her face, and a dreamy look in her eyes. Magnus turned away. He dared not meet her gaze. His own eyes were filling with tears.

The Duke, understanding his feelings, jumped to his feet and said abruptly, 'Sit still, boy. I'm away to stretch my legs.'

Rory stayed behind, looking up at the boy's face, wondering why he was so still, but staying still himself in sympathy. Magnus held the photograph in his trembling hands, staring first at his father's and then at his mother's features till they were both imprinted in his memory.

Tears were trickling down his cheeks, yet there was a warm glow in his heart. At last he had a direct link with his parents. He would keep the photograph to himself and treasure it for ever.

He put it carefully in his pocket and rubbed away the tears with his knuckles. Just in time. The Ferret was kicking the pig's bladder in his direction.

'Come on, Magnus. You can have a kick at it, if you like,' said the boy generously.

'Okay!' Magnus jumped to his feet and took a swipe at the bladder, sending it sailing high into the sky. It was a great kick. He had a feeling that his father and mother were watching and were proud of his prowess.

Chapter 8

THE SPREE

Rainy, rainy rattlestanes,
Dinna rain on me.
Rain on Johnny Groat's hoose,
Far ayont the sea.

The children were having a singing lesson in the little
schoolroom, with Andrew Murray trying his best to
thump out the tune on the tinny piano. Any discords
were drowned by the young voices. Especially Jinty
Cowan's. The Ferret sang louder, but she could beat
him at the high notes, and if she was quick enough she
could get in half a bar ahead of him. It was more like
a race than a song.

Rainy, rainy rattlestanes . . .

It was a suitable enough song, for the rain was rattling on the window-pane like little tapping fingers. But
it would clear up later. Gran had said so, and she was
the best barometer by far on the island. Indeed, the

sun was already beginning to struggle through; and as the rain tailed off Magnus gazed through the window and called out, 'Oh, look!'

The moment he spoke he was annoyed with himself. He had not meant to say it out loud. He was really speaking to himself; but now all the children strained their necks to see what was to be seen.

'It's only a rainbow,' scoffed the Ferret. He had no use for anything so airy-fairy. If it had been a spaceman or a flying saucer, it would have been something worth staring at.

'It's beautiful,' said Andrew, understanding the boy's sudden cry from the heart.

The rainbow hung in a coloured arc over the harbour wall, as if painted on the sky. The pot of gold, if there was one, must be floating in the sea.

The music lesson continued, but Magnus still watched the rainbow, marvelling at the colours and wondering if *he* could ever recapture their beauty. It was a waste of time singing songs when he might have been busy with his paint-brush. He had no ear for a tune, and only pretended to be mouthing the words.

He could always console himself by fingering the treasure in his pocket. He had placed the photograph between two pieces of cardboard to keep it stiff and straight, with an elastic band to secure it. Often, when he was alone, he took out the picture and gazed at his parents. Every day he seemed to know them better.

Speed, bonnie boat, like a bird on the wing . . .

The children were swaying from side to side as they sailed over the sea to Skye. Tair glanced down at his pocket where Avizandum was reminding him of something.

'It's tonight. The spree. Don't forget.'

'No, I'll not forget,' promised Tair, under his breath.

How could he forget? The 'spree' was a jollification organized by the Reverend Alexander Morrison. Everyone on the island had been invited. It was to be held here in the schoolroom, the only hall in Sula, with the desks shoved out of the way, the blackboard turned with its face to the wall, and the hangman's whip firmly locked away for the night.

Any excuse would do for a spree. The Duke's visit, the birth of the McCallum twins, even the pig-killing. There would be singing and dancing and good things to eat; and everyone would be there, including the new babies.

The twins were communal babies. Every household had supplied a 'minding' for them – a knitted shawl, woolly mittens, a pair of bootees. Some had given wooden bowls for their porridge, or horn spoons. Gran, more practical than the rest, helped Mrs McCallum every day with her washing. Small garments flapped about on the line, and Gran ironed them every night with the old box-iron which she heated in the peat fire till it was red hot.

The twins were not likely to lack any comforts. The only problem was the pram. The last one on Sula had been used by Tair himself. It was one which had already been handed on from one family to another, and was in a shaky enough state before it reached him. Now it was pensioned off, like the District Nurse's discarded bicycle. Jinty had wheeled her dolls in it. The Ferret had given himself many a 'hurl' in it. It had been used as a roosting-place by Specky the hen. Gran had wheeled home the peat in it till its wobbly wheels finally gave in. Now it lay propped up against old Cowan's empty pig-sty, so familiar a sight that nobody ever noticed it.

The McCallums had no money for such a major purchase as a new perambulator, especially one suitable for two babies. It was Mr Skinnymalink who solved the problem by setting to work concocting one out of some old crates and boxes. Aided by Magnus, he made a two-seater with six little wheels. It was easy to push or pull, and was a sight worth seeing once Magnus had painted it all over in two cheerful tones: blue for a boy, pink for a girl.

The McCallums were delighted with it, especially Tair who never tired of taking the twins out for an airing. He pushed the pram as solemnly as a grand-father, and was careful not to jerk the babies over the rough road.

Strangely enough, every time he was in charge of his little brother and sister, Avizandum seemed to vanish from Tair's pocket. In vain Tair called out to him, 'Where are you hiding, Avizandum? What's wrong? Say something.' But there was not a sight nor a sound of the creature until the babies were out of the way. Even then Avizandum would be in a grumpy mood. Could it be that he was jealous? Or was Tair himself beginning to grow up?

Tair's biggest problem was trying to keep the new pram away from the Ferret's clutches. Given half a chance he would have toppled the twins out and gone for a hurl in it himself. But Tair always managed to fend him off, especially if Magnus was nearby to protect him.

'If you touch that pram I'll murder you,' Magnus threatened the Ferret one day.

'You and who else!' scoffed the Ferret, kicking out at him. 'I'll bash your head in, Magnus Macduff.'

On the night of the spree all such squabbles were forgotten. The schoolroom looked different in the lamplight, and so did the islanders, all dressed in their best. Even Gran had put on her best blouse and skirt. Plain black, like her serviceable shoes. No brooches or ornaments.

Jinty Cowan made up for it. She had enough beads, bangles and bows for ten. Best of all, she was wearing a pair of high-heeled shoes. How could anyone help admiring her? She preened herself like one of the Duke's peacocks, and took little keeks down at her feet to see that they were still there. Anybody could see that she was the belle of the ball.

The schoolroom, too, was dressed up for the occasion, with bunches of greenery hiding the drabness of the walls, and a trestle-table set out to hold the food. The floor had been sprinkled with soap-powder to make it slippery enough for dancing. The Ferret was already sliding about in his Sunday boots. As for music, old Cowan had unearthed his concertina, which everyone called the squeeze-box, and the minister – a man of many parts – had brought his fiddle.

They were all there, except Mr Skinnymalink who was hovering about outside, looking through the window and then vanishing into the darkness. The tourists looked the sprucest of the lot, with neat bow-ties and their hair well brushed. But it was the twins who were the centre of attraction.

It was difficult to tell which was Rose and which Angus. Each was wrapped up in a shawl, like a dumpling in a cloth, and only their fuzzy red hair could be seen. They were handed round like parcels until everyone had dandled them.

Jinty bounced one of them up and down and sang, 'Ally-bally-bally bee. Sitting on your Mammy's knee.' She envied the baby's flowery name. Fancy Mrs Gillies being called Rose! It didn't suit her one bit, but it suited the baby all right. 'Nice wee Rosebud,' she crooned, snuggling the baby closer.

'It's Angus,' said Mrs McCallum, laughing at her. 'Here! I'll take him from you. He's too heavy.'

There was no formal start to the spree. It just happened. Suddenly old Cowan seized his concertina and began to squeeze out a lively Scottish tune. 'Take your partners,' he shouted, and the next moment they were dancing a rousing Eightsome Reel, kicking up their heels, taking great leaps into the air, and whirling their partners roundabout like peerie-tops.

Jinty tried in vain to persuade Magnus to be her partner, but he dodged out of her way. He was not keen on dancing. All the same, he got some fun out of it, standing in a corner and tripping up the Ferret every time he came clodhopping round.

Sometimes the Ferret was goaded into retaliating. He dashed from the dance, and a flurry of fisticuffs took place in the corner, till Gran dealt Magnus a stinging blow on the side of the head. He accepted it stoically, knowing he deserved it. He rubbed his head, kept

out of her line of vision, and continued to kick the
Ferret whenever he got the chance.

The teacher came and stood beside him. Andrew
would have liked to join the dancers, had it not been
for his lame leg. But there was plenty to watch. The
District Nurse – Rose! – being birled off her feet by
one of the tourists. Jinty Cowan pirouetting in the
middle of the ring, with all her jewels jangling like a
horse's harness. Black Sandy and Morag McCallum
getting mixed up in the Grand Chain. The sweat drop-
ping off old Cowan's brow as he squeezed out *The
Deil Amang The Tailors*.

Andrew glanced at the boy beside him. Magnus was
wearing his Sunday suit. and looked hot and uncom-
fortable, caught in a trap of Harris tweed.

'Why not take off your jacket?' he suggested in a
friendly voice. Most of the men had already shed their
collars and were sweating it out in their shirt-sleeves.
But Magnus stuck stubbornly to his jacket and thrust
his hand into his pocket to make sure his treasure was
safe. He had transferred it to the jacket-pocket of his
good suit rather than leave it at home. Wherever he
went nowadays, the photograph went with him.

'What have you got in your pocket?' Andrew asked
in an amused voice, knowing how often he had to con-
fiscate strange objects from his pupils. In Magnus's
case, it could be anything from a pea-shooter to a field-
mouse.

'Nothing,' said Magnus fiercely, guarding his pocket
as if the teacher meant to rob him. He moved away,
leaving Andrew feeling snubbed, and not for the first
time. Dealing with Magnus was like playing a game of

Snakes and Ladders, one step forward and two back. Still, he felt he was making some progress. The boy had been less difficult lately, especially since the Duke had arrived on the island. Andrew had noticed that the little man seemed to have the power of drawing Magnus out of his shell. Perhaps in time he would emerge from it for good.

As he continued to look on, Andrew felt a great wave of fondness for the island folk. They were his people now, more akin to him than the friends he had left in the mainland. Though he was still an incomer, he was gradually being drawn into the inner circle and becoming an islander himself. The strangeness of being the new schoolmaster had worn off.

He watched Gran laying out the food. The 'spread', they called it. The plates and dishes were spread out on the trestle table which was covered with a white cloth and contained a tempting display of home-made cakes, buns, scones, and sandwiches. There was a big urn of tea, and bottles of home-brewed wine. It was a potent drink, made from rhubarb, dandelions, or wild cherries. *Geans*, they were called on the island. One glass was enough, old Cowan said, to make a bald man's hair curl.

The Reverend Alexander Morrison was in his element, acting as Master of Ceremonies, and getting in as many little jokes as possible, in spite of an accident that had befallen him earlier in the day. He had broken his false teeth. They lay on his desk in the Manse study, wrapped up in a silk handkerchief, awaiting the arrival of the *Hebridean*. The minister had tried a do-it-yourself job of patching them up, but with the first mouth-

ful of hot tea they had come adrift again, leaving him
with a lisp as good as wee Kirsty's.

'It'th no good,' he had told his wife, laying them
aside. 'I'll have to thend them to the dentitht in Cronan.
It'th motht inconvenient.'

Nevertheless it did not stop him from singing his
usual songs at the spree. The Sulans had heard them
dozens of times before, but a spree would not be a spree
without 'The Wee Couper o' Fife' followed by 'The
Laird o' Cockpen' as an encore. The minister lisped
his way through them both and would have repeated
them over again if old Cowan had not struck up a rousing reel.

He had laid aside his concertina and picked up the
fiddle. The strings squeaked, the dancers 'hooched', the
dust flew, the twins yawned in their mother's arms, and
Jinty, leaping like a leprechaun, came down heavily in
her high heels. She limped through the rest of the
dance, paying for her pride with blisters on both heels.
The District Nurse would be busy tomorrow.

Magnus went and stood beside the little Duke who
was tapping out the time with his foot and shouting
'Hooch!' louder than any. But, as old Cowan's discords
grew thicker and faster, he could stand it no longer.
Without a by-your-leave he seized the fiddle from
under the old man's chin, and took over the music.

What a change of tempo and tune! The fiddle-
strings began to sing. The rippling notes chased after
each other in cascades, like little waterfalls of music,
causing the dancers to leap higher and twirl faster. Even
Gran could not keep from jigging from one foot to the
other, while old Cowan, knowing himself defeated,

went and consoled himself with a long drink from the jug on the trestle-table.

The Duke began to make up his own tunes, improvising on the old traditional Scottish airs. Magnus stood watching and listening, fingering the photograph in his pocket, knowing that he was hearing music of a higher quality than had ever been played on the island before.

'What a shame,' he thought to himself with a sudden flash of insight. Why had the Duke kept such wonderful sounds bottled up inside himself? He ought to have shared them with the whole world, as he was sharing them now with the people of Sula. Magnus could see clearly that it was wrong to waste such talent, yet he was blind to the fact that he was wasting his own.

The Duke's face was crinkled with smiles. Beads of perspiration stood out on his brow as his fingers flew faster over the strings, till at last with a final flourish he brought the tune to an end.

'More!' shouted the dancers, jigging about on the slippery floor as if they were wound up and could not stop. 'Encore!'

But Gran shouted 'Food!' In the stampede towards the spread the Ferret was first, stuffing sandwiches into his mouth, grabbing buns with both hands and kicking out at Magnus to prevent him reaching the food.

'I'll punch your nose later,' said Magnus darkly, and went to obey Gran's call of 'Mag-nus! Come and help to pour out the tea.'

It was not so much a matter of pouring out the tea as turning the tap of the sizzling urn and letting the strong brown liquid trickle into the cups. One after the other he filled them, while Jinty acted as his willing hand-maiden, fetching and carrying till everyone was served.

'A thplendid featht,' lisped the minister, dipping a ginger biscuit into his tea to avoid having to chew it.

'I'll have my hands full tomorrow,' prophesied the District Nurse as she watched the Ferret making a dash for the door, holding his stomach. 'Och well! I like to be fully stretched.'

They were all fully stretched by the time the spread was finished. For a while they were content to sit back and be entertained by anyone who would volunteer to do a 'turn'. After much coaxing Tair did a recitation, fixing his eyes on the ceiling and being prompted by Avizandum in his pocket. Then, with no coaxing at all, Jinty took the floor to do a solo dance in her stocking-soles. The tourists sang folk-songs of their own country, after which the Duke struck up a strathspey on the fiddle.

On with the dance. The islanders had found their second wind and would have gone on till dawn. It was not till the oil-lamps began to flicker and the last fiddle-string broke that Gran called a halt.

'That's it! It's high time we were all in our beds.'

The twins were sleeping peacefully in their mother's arms. The District Nurse hoisted up her namesake and said, 'Home to beddy-byes. Magnus, fetch the pram.'

The two-seater had been parked outside the school-room door. Magnus went out and took a deep breath of cool air. It was neither night nor morning. A great stillness lay over Sula. Not even the whirr of a bird's wing could be heard.

Magnus stiffened as he caught sight of a stealthy

figure in the distance. At the same time he noticed that the pram was missing. The Ferret had taken possession of it and was steering it down the zig-zag path towards the harbour.

'Stop!' shouted Magnus, rushing after him, seething with anger. Too late. The Ferret swerved into the harbour wall. There was an ominous crash, and the Hermit's patient work was ruined. The two-seater fell apart. The wheels went careering down into the water, and the painted woodwork was smashed to smithereens.

The Ferret picked himself up and ran off into the darkness like a hunted hare, hoping to save his skin. Black with rage, Magnus pursued him. There was no thought of mercy in his heart; only revenge. He would fight the Ferret, and this time it would not be in fun, but in earnest.

Suddenly, as he chased after his quarry, he saw something gleaming in the moonlight. It was the pig's bladder lying outside the Ferret's door.

'I'll burst it!' cried Magnus, searching in his pocket for a safety-pin. He would make the Ferret suffer in more ways than one. The loss of the bladder would have a more lasting effect on the culprit than a black eye.

As he plunged the pin into the skin and heard the sigh of air when the bladder burst, he had a feeling of exaltation. Revenge was sweet. Yet in his heart he knew it was also silly. He had taken the bounce out of the balloon, but revenge had a habit of bouncing back.

Chapter 9

REVENGE

'Where's Magnus?'

The little Duke came down to the row of houses at the harbour, searching for his young friend. He had been humming to himself as he walked – or rather pranced – down the path, making music in his head.

All the sounds of Sula were there: the cry of the sea-birds, the bleating of sheep, the moaning of the wind, the thud of surf swishing against the boats, the excited babble of children's voices. He would blend them all into a new symphony, to play to himself in his tower when he got home to Cronan Castle.

At the sound of his voice Rory got up from old Cowan's doorstep and went to meet him, wagging his tail.

'Hullo, old fellow,' said the Duke, stooping to pat the collie's rough coat. 'Where's Magnus?'

The dog trotted ahead of him towards Gran's cottage. A small queue of children stood outside, waiting and listening.

'What's up? What are you waiting for?' asked the Duke, joining the queue.

'Wheesht!' said Tair, cocking his ear to listen. He and the rest of the children had long got over their awe of the Duke. Even Jinty had stopped curtseying to him. He was just a man, a wee bit queer at times, but they liked him. 'Wheesht!' repeated Tair. 'It's nearly ready.'

'What's nearly ready?'

'Listen!' said Tair, as if that was enough explanation.

The Duke cocked his ear like the rest, and heard a swish-swishing sound from inside. For a moment he was puzzled. Then his face crinkled into smiles as an old, half-forgotten memory came back to him. Gran was making butter. The sound he heard was the swish of the cream slapping against the sides of the wooden churn as she turned the handle with a slow and steady rhythm.

The children could tell by the sound when the butter was ready to come. The tune changed from swish-swish to thud-thud. A few more turns of the creaking handle and the job was done.

Tair licked his lips in anticipation. Avizandum peered out of his pocket and whispered, 'You'll soon be getting a drink of buttermilk.'

'Buttermilk? You mean soor-dook,' said Tair, who had lately taken to contradicting his familiar.

'Same thing,' said Avizandum sharply. 'Some say buttermilk. Some say soor-dook.'

'*I* say soor-dook,' said Tair firmly, and heard no more from Avizandum for the rest of that day.

It was the children's treat when Gran, or anyone else on Sula, was making butter. They enjoyed the refreshing drink with its tangy taste, and the white moustache it left on their lips afterwards.

Magnus came to the door bearing a jug full to the brim of frothy liquid.

'Soor-dook!' he called out.

'Me first!'

The children crowded round him, trying to push their way to the front. The Duke in the background found himself as eager as the rest to taste it. 'It's years since I've had a drink of buttermilk,' he told Magnus in an excited voice. 'Years and years and years.'

'Wait! I'll fetch a glass,' said Magnus; but the little Duke shook his head.

'No, no, I want it from the jug,' he said, and waited for his turn as patiently as he could. When the jug reached him, he took a deep drink and smacked his lips. 'It tastes like nectar,' he declared, turning up his eyes to the sky.

Neither he nor any of the others had ever tasted nectar, but they all nodded their heads in agreement. Soor-dook, buttermilk, nectar, what did the name matter? They drained the jug to the last drop, and wiped off their moustaches with the backs of their hands.

The only one missing was the Ferret who was hiding round the corner, thirsting for a drink of soor-dook but stubbornly keeping out of sight. He was thirsting, too, for revenge. He had been in a strange sulky mood ever since the night of the spree. He still bore a bump on his brow, but he was not so much worried about the punch-up he had received from Magnus, as the loss of his pig's bladder.

The fight had been fair, but violent. Thumps, kicks, and blows were exchanged on both sides. The Ferret had given Magnus a black eye, but that was nothing to the punishment he had received. His nose had bled, his shins were bruised, there were cuts and bumps on his brow. It was a fight to the finish, and he had lost.

Fair enough. He had observed his defeat. He felt no resentment towards the victor, not until he discovered the loss of his football. It was then that his wounds really began to hurt, and he determined at all costs to get his own back.

He watched and waited and brooded and spied. He saw Magnus walking away with the little Duke down towards the rocks. Looking for the seals, likely. Old Whiskers! The Ferret's eyes narrowed. Maybe he could hurt Magnus through the seals. He would hurt him in some way. Wait, and his chance would come.

It came next day when they were at school. Even there, and in the playground, the Ferret turned his back on Magnus and refused to be drawn into a friendly wrestling match. For his part, Magnus was willing to forgive and forget. The fight was over and the incident forgotten, as far as he was concerned. He had helped Mr Skinnymalink to make a new two-seater for the twins, patching up the remains of the old one as best they could. The Ferret watched them furtively from a distance.

'If you touch this, I'll murder you,' Magnus shouted

at him, but it was only a friendly threat. 'You can come and help, if you like,' he added.

Nothing doing. The Ferret slunk away without even sticking his tongue out at Magnus. Today he sat brooding at his desk, his catapult lying untouched in front of him. The teacher had drawn a map of Scotland on the blackboard, and was filling in the towns, asking the children where to place them.

'Edinburgh. Glasgow. Aberdeen. Stirling.'

Jinty knew the lot, and told him in her smug voice.

'Cronan,' said Andrew Murray, pausing with the chalk in his hand.

Once more Jinty was ready with her answer, but the teacher ignored it. 'Magnus,' he called out. 'You know where Cronan is. You've been there. Come out and show us on the map.'

He had to speak several times before the boy heard him. Magnus was away in a world of his own. He had been doodling on his jotter, drawing a fox on its hind-legs and a solan goose sailing across the sky. He was not thinking about what he was drawing but about the photograph in his pocket.

He felt an urge to look at it again. He took it out and laid it carefully on the desk. His parents looked up at him, smiling. They seemed closer than ever. His own flesh and blood.

'Magnus!'

'What?'

'Come out at once.'

'Yessir.'

Magnus had no time to put the photograph back in his pocket. All he could do was hide it hastily under his jotter. But the Ferret had seen out of the corner of his eye. He had known for some time that Magnus was keeping something secret in his pocket. Now was his chance to find out what it was, and to get his revenge. Swiftly, while Magnus's back was turned, he reached out and took the picture.

Andrew Murray was handing the chalk to Magnus. 'Now, Magnus, mark Cronan on the map.'

Magnus took the chalk and stared at the blackboard. The map was a lifeless-looking thing. He would sooner have drawn Old Whiskers than bothered about putting towns in their right places.

'It's there,' he said, marking a cross more or less in the correct place. He did not want to think of Cronan with its noise and turmoil. He wanted to get back to his desk so that he could rescue his precious photograph; but the teacher was not finished with him yet.

'Tell us something about it, Magnus. What was Cronan like?' he asked, determined to draw him out. It was time the boy learnt to express himself other than through his drawings. 'Come along, give us a description of the town.'

Magnus gave him a look. What on earth did the man want him to say? How could he describe Cronan? It was only a cross on the blackboard.

He shuffled his feet and said, 'It was a great muckle big place.'

Andrew waited. 'What else?' he asked patiently.

'Nothing.'

'Oh well,' sighed the teacher, giving it up, 'you'd better go back to your seat.'

Magnus went, keeping a wary eye on the Ferret in

case he tripped him up as he went past. But he was too busy tearing something into small shreds of paper. He looked up as Magnus went past and gave him a strange sly smile. They were quits now.

Magnus slid into his seat and lifted up his jotter to find the photograph. It was not there. His face went white. His hands began to tremble. He swayed in his seat as the awful truth dawned on him. The Ferret had torn his parents into little pieces which could never be put together again. His only link with the past was gone for ever.

The Ferret whipped round and shot him a triumphant glance. But when he saw the stricken look on Magnus's face he shrank back as if he had been hit by a blow. Had he gone too far? He had got his revenge, there was no doubt about that, but would Magnus ever forgive him?

Magnus was not even looking at him. He did not seem to be seeing or hearing anything. There was a blank look in his eyes, and his trembling had given place to a strange stillness.

'What's wrong, Magnus?' asked Jinty in a worried whisper. 'Are you not well?'

It would be an unheard of thing if Magnus was ill. He had never even had the measles. But something was certainly wrong with him now. All the blood had drained from his face and he seemed suddenly to have turned to stone.

Andrew, too, had noticed, and came limping towards him. 'Is there anything the matter, Magnus?' he asked, in a voice full of concern, and laid a hand on the boy's arm.

At his touch Magnus came to life. He sprang up from his seat, swept past the teacher, and dashed out of the door leaving everyone gaping.

Trix, the teacher's small dog, was lying outside the door. She gave a friendly bark and leapt up to be patted, but Magnus did not see her. Nor did he notice Rory spread-eagled at old Cowan's door. He went straight past and into Gran's cottage.

It was empty, save for Specky pecking about on the kitchen floor. Magnus went up the steep stairs to his bedroom and shut the door. He sat down on his bed. His body was rigid, his fists were tightly clenched; his mind, too, seemed to be locked.

He could not analyse what he was feeling. If it had been merely anger he could have fought the Ferret and that would have been the end of it. But fighting would not relieve the ache at his heart, nor bring his father and mother back.

He sat there in the stillness trying to recall their features. Suddenly his eyes focused on his paint-box. The black look left his face. An idea was forming in his mind. He had never succeeded in drawing humans before, only animals and birds. But this was different. At least, he could try.

He took up his drawing-book and set to work, but his hands were trembling so much that he could scarcely hold the pencil steady. He drew a few shaky lines, then scored them out in disgust and tore up the paper. Again and again he tried, but the faces refused to appear. Then, out of custom, he drew a background of sea and seagulls and seals. Suddenly he could see the faces more clearly. His father was gazing straight at him. His mother was smiling, with a dreamy look in her eyes. If only he could capture them on paper . . .

He did not hear the shouts of the children coming home from school, nor the swish of the sea splashing against the rocks. The waves were growing wilder and the air had become sharp and cold, but Magnus was too absorbed to notice.

Gran was calling, 'Mag-nus! Mag-nus!' in a cross voice. She had to climb the stairs and rattle on the door before he heard her.

He pushed the drawing under the bed and followed her down to the kitchen. He was still in a strange state of turmoil, not knowing what he was feeling. When Gran handed him a basket he stared at it stupidly and said, 'What's that?'

'It's some butter and scones,' she said sharply. 'Take them to the tourists, and warn them to watch their tent. The weather's changing.'

Gran knew about weather as she knew instinctively about so many things. True enough, Magnus felt a nip in the air when he went outside. He saw how the rowan tree in the Manse garden was bending in the breeze, with its red berries swaying. The boats were rocking in the water; there would be no fishing tonight.

Old Cowan spoke to him. He had his coat collar turned up, and was off with Rory at his heels and his crook in his hand to round up his sheep.

'Ay, Magnus, the days are drawing in.'

Magnus could picture the days drawing in, curling up like a piece of bacon in the frying-pan. He noticed that the sharper colours of autumn were replacing the soft shades of summer. Burnt-brown bracken, bronze leaves, red berries, purple heather. It was the best time of year, the boy thought; yet any time of the year was the best on Sula.

The dark mood began to leave him as he walked towards the tourists' tent. The thought of the picture he had drawn was bringing a feeling of consolation to him, though he knew it could never replace the lost photograph. It was only when he saw the Ferret crouching behind the empty pig-sty that the black feeling came back.

He would never speak to the Ferret again. Never. He would not even fight him. He was finished with the Ferret for ever. For the first time in his life Magnus was feeling real hatred in his heart.

He marched past, looking neither to right nor to left. The Ferret watched him through his sandy lashes. He was holding a handful of sticky burrs to throw at anyone who passed. In normal times he would have flung them at Magnus, but not now.

The Ferret was at a loss to know how to deal with Magnus. He wanted to make a friendly gesture. But what? There was only one thing he had which Magnus would like to own. His catapult. It would be a wrench to part with it, but anything was better than this breach with his friend.

Sven and Bjorn were tightening their tent-pegs when Magnus reached them. The canvas was flapping in the gusty wind, and they had foreseen the change in the weather. No need to warn them. Magnus handed over the basket, and Sven said, 'Very grateful. Please thank the good grandmother.'

Magnus waited till he went inside and emptied the basket.

'We go soon, when the boat comes,' said Bjorn, still busy with the guy-ropes. 'It is good here, but we must return to our own country.'

'Going away!' said Magnus, feeling suddenly sorry that they were leaving. The tourists had fitted in to life on Sula, without causing any trouble. They would leave a gap. He began to regret that he had not found out more about their paintings.

Bjorn seemed to read his thoughts. 'We take many pictures away in our heads,' he said, gazing around at the windswept island. 'Many pictures to paint when we get home. Also we leave one here.'

'Where?' asked Magnus, but he guessed that the little Duke had bought it.

'The small lordship, he buy it from us. Ja, ja! He also tell us about you, Mag-nus, that some day you will be the famous painter. So we want to leave behind to you a present. Sven, you bring it from the tent.'

'Ja, I bring it.'

Sven emerged from the tent carrying a canvas under his arm.

'For you, Mag-nus. You will paint the good picture on it.'

Magnus's face flushed with pleasure at the thought of the picture he would paint, a real picture, not just a daub in a drawing-book. It would be a portrait of his parents, with enough room for a background of seals and sea-birds. It was not easy for him to accept anything gracefully, yet he managed to say 'Thanks' with a genuine warmth in his voice.

'Wait.' Sven dived back into the tent and brought out Gran's basket. He had filled it with odds and ends that might be of use to Magnus; half-empty bottles of turps and oil, a palette knife, old rags, a paint brush and some tubes of paint. 'For you, Mag-nus to help with the pictures.'

The boy could only gulp with pleasure, but the men understood and beamed at him, glad to know that they had done something to make him happy.

Magnus hurried back home and hid his spoil under the bed. He would have liked to stay in his room and begin his painting straight away. But Gran was shouting 'Mag-nus! Mag-nus!' in an insistent voice.

There were a dozen jobs to do: the day's washing to deliver to Mrs McCallum, the cow to feed, peat to bring in, driftwood to gather – and all the time the sky was darkening, the wind rising, and the sea splashing in over the harbour wall.

His final task was to carry a can of milk to the school-master. The Ferret came running after him, with his catapult in his hand and his carrotty hair blown upright in the breeze.

'Wait, Magnus, I've got something for you,' he called out breathlessly. Magnus went steadily on, pushing against the wind. He heard, though he paid no atten-tion; but the Ferret was not to be thwarted. He was determined to make his great sacrifice, and put an end to this miserable feud. He ran past Magnus, then turned to bar his way.

'Here, Magnus, you can have my catapult,' he said, thrusting it at him. It never entered his head that Magnus would refuse such a generous offer. *He* would have grabbed it at once.

He was more surprised than hurt when Magnus ignored the offer, gave him a silent push and went on his way without a single word.

Indignation took over. 'You're a silly sumph,' shouted the Ferret, stooping to pick up a pebble. It would be war to the end, if that was the way Magnus wanted it. He took aim with the rejected catapult. Ping! The pebble hit the milk-can, but even then Magnus showed no reaction. He went steadily on till he was out of reach, and what he was thinking, the Ferret would never know.

They lit the lamps in the schoolhouse earlier than usual. True enough, the days were drawing in. Magnus could see the teacher sitting by the fireside reading, with the little dog Trix on his knee. At the table two men were poring over the draught-board, looking as serious as if they were plotting a battle instead of playing a game. The Duke and Mr Skinnymalink were engaged in a silent battle of wits. They enjoyed each other's company, these two, but made no demands on each other.

The Hermit was becoming less solitary, though there were still times when he preferred to live in a hut or a cave rather than in a house. Indeed, as the game ended, he pushed his chair back and left the room. He passed Magnus without speaking and melted away into the darkness; but the boy understood. He and Mr Skinnymalink respected each other's silent moods.

The Duke came out, too, for a breath of air, but there was nothing silent about him. He clapped his hands like a child when he saw Magnus, and cried, 'Good! I've been wanting to see you, boy. Come for a walk. Wait, I'll take in the milk, then we'll go and get the cobwebs blown away.'

The little Duke was nearly blown away himself. He had to cling to Magnus's arm to steady himself. 'It's years since I've been out in such a gale,' he gasped. 'Years and years. Can you hear the music in the wind?'

'Yes, I can,' said Magnus, understanding how the Duke heard sounds in the same way that he saw pictures. The waves were crashing over the harbour wall like an orchestra in full fling; roofs were rattling like tympany; the wind was whistling a thin shrill tune. Magnus gulped in the salty air. His own troubles were being blown away by the gale.

The Duke had a problem of his own. As they were passing the tourists' tent he turned to Magnus and said, 'There's something I want to tell you, boy.'

'I know,' said Magnus. 'You've bought their picture.'

'For you, as a parting gift. That's what I'm trying to tell you. I'm going away.'

Magnus stopped and stared at the Duke through the half-darkness. He felt suddenly bereft, as if the ground had given way under his feet. 'When?'

'When the boat comes. I wish I could stay here for ever, but I have to get back to Cronan. All the same, I've got a plan, boy. Listen.'

But Magnus felt too numb to listen. There was no more music in the wind, only discords.

Chapter 10

RESCUE

Old Whiskers was turning somersaults in the sea. Not because he was feeling frisky; he was doing it against his will. The waves were tossing him up-and-under until he felt as light-headed as a minnow.

He was looking for the young seals. Silly things, they thought it was fun to get tossed and tumbled in the stormy sea. He knew better. Before long the waves would be too strong for them. They would exhaust themselves, then be in danger of being dashed against the rocks.

He sniffed and snorted and grunted at them, trying to round them up and lead them to safety.

'This way. Follow me. Hurry!'

At last he attracted their attention and led the way through the churning sea to calmer waters round the point. Little Sula was gradually being swamped by the waves. Soon it would be lost from sight.

The young seals came after him, battered by the sea and feeling less sprightly now. They would be glad to reach a sheltered haven. After all, Old Whiskers knew what was best for them.

The old seal ploughed steadily on. He thought of the boy, but he knew that Magnus would not come seeking him on such a stormy day. Wait till the weather was calmer and they would be together again.

At that moment the boy was thinking of Old Whiskers. He had locked himself into his bedroom so that he could work undisturbed on his new canvas. He felt a thrill of excitement as he worked. He was a real painter now.

The picture, copied from the one he had thrust under the bed, was taking shape. The faces of his father and mother were coming to life, almost as real as in the photograph. Now he was finishing off the background – the birds and animals he had drawn in at the start.

For hours he had been painting, locked away in his own world. He had switched off, so that he was unaware of the school bell, the howling wind, the crashing waves, and Gran's angry shouts of 'Mag-nus.'

The wind had abated during the night, but only to gather its forces. Now it was whipping itself up into a fury, battering against doors, rattling the windows, tossing the waves high over the harbour wall.

The tourists' tent had been blown from its moorings, and the men had found refuge in the Manse. The loose slates on the schoolroom roof were making as much din as if they were doing a clog-dance.

'Where's Magnus Macduff?'

It was a question the teacher often had to ask when marking the register.

'Please, sir, he's not here,' said Jinty Cowan, always the first to answer.

'I can see that for myself,' said Andrew Murray sharply. 'I'm asking if anyone knows where he is.'

Jinty would dearly have loved to say that she knew, but she had not seen him all morning. She had hovered outside Gran's door in the hope that she might walk to school with him, not side-by-side, but a few paces behind, like a faithful dog. But Magnus had not appeared.

'He could be anywhere,' she told the teacher helpfully.

'He could not,' said Tair, prompted by Avizandum. 'He couldn't be on the moon. Nor he couldn't be in fairyland. Nor he couldn't be . . .'

'That'll do, Tair,' said the teacher sternly, and went on marking the register.

There was another absentee. The Ferret was missing from his place; but this time Jinty was luckier. She could give chapter and verse about his movements.

'Please, sir, one of Gran's sheep's missing, and she was going to send Magnus to look for it, but she couldn't find him, so she sent the Ferret instead. Up the Heathery Hill. He hasn't come back yet.'

'So I see. Thank you, Jinty. Now, settle down and open your books.'

But how could they settle down with the clog-dance going on overhead and the gale gusting against the windows?

'Please, sir.' Once more Jinty had her hand up.

'Yes, Jinty, what is it now?'

She stood up, ready to make an announcement. 'Please, sir, it's awful stormy.'

'I know that,' said Andrew impatiently. 'Sit down.'

Jinty stayed on her feet. She had not said her say yet. 'Please, sir, my mother says the *Hebridean* won't get in today, and the tourists won't get away, and neither will His Lordship, and the minister won't get his teeth mended, and please, sir, Miss Macfarlane used to give us a holiday when it was stormy.'

So that was it. Having delivered her speech Jinty looked round for acclaim, and got it. The others shuffled their feet. It was as good as a round of applause. As for Andrew, he felt like shouting to her to shut up. Instead, he said firmly, 'Sit down, Jinty,' and made no other comment.

He was tired of hearing Miss Macfarlane quoted at him. He had been considering sending the children home, but he was not going to let Jinty think she had given him the idea. She was smug enough already.

She was right, of course. Andrew looked out of the window and saw that the waves were splashing as far up as the cottage doors. The *Hebridean* would never make the harbour in such a storm.

He was glad in one way. It would mean that the Duke would stay longer. He and the Hermit could continue their silent games of draughts in the evenings. The tourists, too, would be welcome to stay. As for food supplies, there was plenty of meal and flour and potatoes on the island. It was the extras they would miss – the treats of sausages and butcher's meat and baker's buns – and there would be no letters and newspapers. All the same, there was a certain excitement in the prospect of being storm-bound, like a castaway on a desert island.

A sudden gust rattled against the panes and almost blew the window in.

'That's it,' said Andrew, making up his mind. 'Class dismiss.'

The children needed no second telling. They were on their feet and at the door before he could change his mind. Jinty preened herself as if they had her to thank.

'Cheerio, sir,' she said brightly. 'If I see Magnus or the Ferret, I'll tell them not to bother to come.'

Andrew ignored her, and gave a warning to the others. 'Go straight home. No playing about outside; and keep away from the harbour. It's not safe.'

'Yessir.'

They knew better than he did. They had been through dozens of storms before, and could weather them without any fuss. It was all part of life on Sula. Take the bad with the good.

Magnus, too, was becoming aware of the storm. The sky was darkening and the daylight fading so that he could scarcely see what he was painting, but by now he had almost finished. He propped the canvas up on the old dressing table and stood back to look at it.

It was not perfect. The birds and animals pleased him. They looked better on the canvas than in his drawing-book; but he was not so sure about his parents. He did not know what their colouring had been like in real life. Was his mother's hair yellow and her eyes blue? He had given his father brown eyes, and dark-brown hair with a russet gleam in it. He had tried hard, too, to get a weather-beaten look in his cheeks.

Magnus realized how much he had still to find out, not only about his parents, but about how to apply paint to canvas. He knew at the back of his mind that the little Duke was right. On the windy walk last night Magnus had been only half-listening to him. Now he recalled some of the conversation.

'I've got a plan. Come to Cronan and stay with me in the Castle. There's another room in the Tower. You could paint pictures there, and get lessons at the High School. And I could make music. We could help each other . . .'

The words had been blown away by the gale, yet Magnus recalled the note of sadness in the Duke's voice as he continued, 'Don't waste your life, boy. Look at me. I've come to nothing. I might have made something of my music, but I've frittered it away.' He clutched at the boy's arm. 'Perhaps it's not too late. If you come to Cronan, who knows what we might both do . . .'

It was true. Perhaps they could help each other. The little man in the lonely castle needed someone to share his thoughts and feelings. Magnus, too, was lost in a maze with no means of communication except through his drawing. The Duke was the only human being to whom he could talk freely.

A handful of pebbles rattled against the window-pane, the familiar signal from the Ferret when he wanted to entice Magnus out for a game or a fight. At first Magnus made no response. He was still feeling bitter against the Ferret. Let him rattle away. He would stick to his resolve never to speak to him again.

The rattling continued, and at last Magnus realized that the pebbles were not being flung by any human hand. The wind was tossing them against the window-pane. He looked out and saw the clouds scudding across the sky, the waves swamping the boats, the spindrift swirling up to the very doorsteps.

He could see Jinty prancing from foot to foot in her wellington boots, like a wet hen. She was clutching her wind-blown hair and shrieking up at Magnus, trying to attract his attention.

'Magnus. Come down. Something's happened.'

'What? I can't hear you.'

'Wait. I'll come up and tell you.'

'No!'

Magnus was out of his bedroom in a flash before she could invade his privacy. He ran down the stairs, jump-ing the last few steps. Jinty met him at the bottom and launched into her story.

'Isn't it a terrible storm? The teacher sent us home from school. I told him! And d'you know what? The Ferret wasn't there. He's lost.'

'Lost? How could he be lost?'

'He is so lost. Everybody's been looking for him. He's not anywhere.'

Magnus stared at her. 'Where did he go?' he asked, still not believing her.

'Up the Hill. Gran sent him up to look for one of her sheep. She was trying to get hold of you, Magnus, but she couldn't find you. So the Ferret went, and he never came back. Isn't it terrible?'

She rolled her eyes like a tragedy queen, but Magnus

had already pushed past her, out into the teeth of the gale. He did not notice the storm. He could only think that if anything had happened to the Ferret, it was his fault. If he had not been so selfishly absorbed in his painting he would have heard Gran's calls of 'Magnus!' All the bitterness he had felt faded away. Now that he was missing, Magnus realized how fond he was of the Ferret.

Old Cowan, bent half-double in the wind, was making his way home, clutching his crook.

'I've given up. He's nowhere to be seen.'

He had found Gran's missing ewe, but not the Ferret. Rory was at his heels, tired after his long trek up the Heathery Hill and ready to follow his master into the house. When he saw Magnus he hesitated.

'I'll go and have another look,' said the boy, and made off in the direction of the Hill.

'Watch yourself,' old Cowan shouted after him. 'You might get blown away. You're wasting your time.'

He was wasting his words. Magnus plodded on alone, but only for a few steps. Before long he heard Rory panting behind him.

'Good dog,' said Magnus, stopping to pat him. 'Come on. We'll find the Ferret.'

It was comforting to have a friendly creature with him. Together they stumbled up the Hill in the teeth of the gale. The higher they climbed the more the wind buffeted them. The bracken was bent to the ground. Even the sturdy heather seemed in danger of being tugged from its roots. There was no bird to be seen; they were all hiding in nooks and crannies on the cliffs.

Half-way up Magnus stopped to draw his breath and

looked back at the storm-tossed island. There was
something magnificent and exciting about the scene.
Terrifying, too; as if a giant was flying over Sula, shouting, 'I'll huff and I'll puff and I'll blow the place down.'

Smoke from the chimneys was doing a crazy dance
across the sky. The few trees on the island were bent
almost double, like old men with sore backs. The sea
was full of spume and spray and galloping white horses.
There was no sign of Little Sula lost under the swirling
water. Magnus hoped that Old Whiskers had found a
safe refuge.

The air was filled with crashing sounds, like one of
the Duke's stormy symphonies. With such competition,
it was useless trying to shout for the Ferret. Magnus
and the dog slipped and slithered as they made their
way round to the cave where the Hermit sometimes
took refuge. It was empty except for a heap of coloured
stones gleaming in the half-light. For a time they took
shelter there, while Magnus thought of his next move.
He did not take long to make up his mind.

'Stay there, Rory. I'm going to look over the cliff.'

It was a dangerous move to make in such a high gale.
It would be all too easy for him to lose his balance and
be swept down to the rocks. Rory, too, could be bowled
over by the wind; but he was not going to be left behind. When he saw where the boy was going, he ran on
ahead and stood panting at the edge of the cliff, brac-
ing himself to withstand the force of the storm.

All of a sudden the hairs on his body stiffened and
he let out a short sharp yelp.

'What is it, Rory? Have you seen something?'

The boy was at his side, peering over the cliff, and

struggling to keep his balance. The dog had seen something on the shore, where Magnus had found the carrageen moss. A heap of driftwood? A dead seal? Or the body of the Ferret?

The waves were coming crashing in, nearer and nearer. Soon they would swallow up the inert object, as Little Sula had been swamped by the sea.

'I'm going down,' said Magnus.

He had a cold feeling at his heart. Fear and remorse. If the Ferret was dead, he had killed him. Rory stood helplessly watching as Magnus disappeared over the cliff-edge. The boy clung to anything he could find to brake his descent: a handful of sea-pinks, a jutting rock, a clump of heather. But it was not enough. He lost has balance and fell, rolling over and over like a barrel, down to the very edge of the sea.

A wave splashed over him. Magnus struggled to his feet, bruised but with no bones broken. The Ferret had not been so lucky. He lay doubled up, soaked with spray, and with blood on his brow. His face was ashen pale, but as Magnus bent over him, he heard a faint moan. The Ferret was still alive.

The relief was so great that Magnus gave a shout of joy. Then, as another wave splashed in, he came back to reality. They would both be drowned unless he took some quick action. There was no hope of being rescued by boat. He would have to carry the Ferret up the cliff,

It would be no easy matter hoisting a dead-weight up the crumbling cliff. Magnus was afraid he might hurt the Ferret. Afraid, too, lest he lost his footing. It needed only one false step, and they would both be swept into the angry sea.

He set his teeth and stooped to pick up his burden. The Ferret stirred and half-opened his eyes. 'It's okay,' said Magnus. 'Hang on and you'll be all right.'

The Ferret gave a kind of grunt and then went limp in Magnus's arms. The wind was howling like a pack of hungry wolves as Magnus started his perilous climb. He looked up and saw Rory standing at the top like a sentinel, watching. It was comforting to know that he was not alone, even though the dog could do nothing to help.

Yet there *was* something. Rory sensed the danger and suddenly knew what he must do. He must hurry home and raise the alarm, so that Old Cowan could follow him back to the cliff-top. Another pair of hands was needed to haul Magnus and the Ferret to safety.

The dog gave a yelp as if to announce his intentions, then set off to fight his way home against the wind. Magnus half-heard him. He was concentrating on every foothold, trying to carry the Ferret in one arm and cling with his free hand to anything he could find.

The gale blew harder, his burden grew heavier, and his strength was fast fading away. 'Come on, Magnus; come on,' he kept telling himself. 'One more step, then another, and another . . .'

It was the most wonderful sight in the world – the light in Gran's window. Soon he would be safely home. It was wonderful too, to know that the Ferret was alive and in good hands. Mrs Gillies had already taken charge of him, and he was now fast asleep, wrapped in warm blankets.

'His ankle's broken, and it'll be touch and go whether

he takes pneumonia, but I'll pull him round,' she said with a gleam in her eye.

The District Nurse would pull him round all right, but it was Magnus who had saved the Ferret's life, though not alone. Rory, stumbling with weariness, was still at the boy's heels. He would wait until he saw Magnus safely home before taking his own well-earned rest in old Cowan's cottage.

When Magnus was making his last desperate effort to reach the top of the cliff, he found helping hands waiting to take over his burden. Old Cowan was there, along with Mr Skinnymalink and the little Duke. Without them, the Ferret would not be lying snug in his bed. It would have taken Magnus hours – exhausted as he was – to carry him home by himself.

Now at last he reached his own doorstep and turned to dismiss the dog. 'It's all right now, Rory. Go home.'

Magnus could picture the scene inside. Gran would be bustling about the kitchen, perhaps breaking a piece of peat to put on the fire, or scalding out a milk-pail. Anything but sitting idle. There would be something cooking in a pot by the fire, perhaps stovies, or potatoes boiled in their jackets. It would be a relief to get in out of the gale and revive himself with a hot meal.

He opened the door and stood blinking in the lamplight, like a pit pony. When he saw Gran he blinked again in disbelief. She was sitting on one of the hard chairs, staring into space, with her hands folded in her lap.

The kettle was spitting over on to the hearth, but Gran took no notice of it. There was a different look on her face, softer and sadder, and something was glistening in her eyes. Surely not tears. What could be wrong? Was she weeping because of the Ferret?

'It's all right, Gran,' he said hastily. 'The Ferret's fine. We've found him.'

She did not seem to hear. A tear trickled slowly down her wrinkled cheek, the first Magnus had ever seen her shed, but she did not even wipe it away.

The boy forgot his own weariness. He went white with alarm and cried out, 'What's wrong, Gran? Are you ill?'

Now at last she looked at him. 'I've seen it,' she said in a shaky voice.

Magnus went even whiter. What had Gran seen? A ghost? But Gran, who could face any man or beast without flinching, was not likely to be frightened by anything.

'I've seen it,' she repeated, blinking away another tear. 'In your bedroom.'

And then he knew! Gran *had* seen a ghost. Two ghosts. Her son and his wife propped up against the old dressing-table in his room.

'Oh, Gran!'

He could imagine the shock it must have been to her when she opened the door and saw the picture facing her. How bewildered she must have been, and what memories must have come flooding back to her as she stood staring at her dead son and the young girl he had married.

The old woman had bottled up her emotions for so long. Now she had no means of expressing herself. She sat staring at Magnus, with unasked questions on her lips. How had he came to paint such a picture? How could he have known what his parents looked like?

At last she spoke in a faltering voice. 'How did you know?'

'Oh, Gran!'

Magnus was as speechless as the old woman. For the first time in his life he longed to break down the barriers between them. If he could speak freely to the little Duke, surely he could find a way of communicating with Gran, his own flesh and blood.

He made a brave try. 'It was a photograph, Gran,' he burst out. 'The Duke gave it to me, but the Ferret tore it up, so I tried to paint them so that I could remember what they looked like.'

It was the longest speech he had ever made to Gran. Never before had she sat still and listened quietly to him. But he was not finished yet. He tried to tell her how he felt when he first saw the photograph, and how he had always wanted to find out about his parents.

'Tell me about them, Gran,' he pleaded. He knew this was a moment that might never be repeated. Gran must talk now before she shut herself up again. They both must. 'Please tell me, Gran. What were they like?'

She looked at the boy as if she was seeing her dead son instead of Magnus.

'He was a good laddie,' she said quietly. 'The lassie was all right, too. Ay, they were a fine pair. The laddie was a great one for climbing the cliffs and watching the sea-birds. And the seals, too; just like you. He never wanted to leave Sula. When he went to the fishing he was always in a hurry to get home. I used to watch for him, sailing back round Sula Point.'

Her voice faltered again, and she gripped her hands

together to steady herself. 'There was one morning when the boat didn't come back.'

'I know, Gran.'

Magnus went forward and laid a hand on her shoulder. It was only a light touch, but it brought the tears flooding to the old woman's eyes.

'My poor laddie,' she sobbed, but whether she was talking about her son or about himself Magnus could not tell. He could only stand there feeling helpless. And yet glad, too. Gran was at last showing some human feeling. It would be better for them both if only they could break down the barriers.

She looked up at him through her tears and for the first time seemed to see that the boy was wet and cold and bruised after his ordeal on the cliff.

'Sit down,' she said in her old sharp way. 'I'll get you something to eat.' She rose from her seat and wiped her eyes on her apron.

Magnus had forgotten his weariness till he sank down on the chair she had vacated. His bones ached, his mind was in a turmoil, but the glow from the peat-fire brought a comforting warmth to his body. There was a warm feeling, too, in his heart when he looked at Gran and thought of what had happened.

She was stumping about the kitchen, stirring the stovies in the pan, setting out the dishes, and looking much the same as usual except for a redness at her eyes. He saw her plainly now – a lone figure, self-sufficient like himself, and like himself, with a vulnerable spot in her heart. Self-sufficiency was not enough for either of them. Life had to be shared; and the first thing he could share with Gran was the picture.

He looked round the kitchen at the blank walls with no other adornment than an old sheep-dip calendar. Suddenly he sat up in his chair and said, 'Gran.'

'What?' She half-turned, holding the wooden spoon which she was using to stir the stovies.

He pointed to the blank space above the mantel-piece. 'We could hang the picture there, Gran. If you like.'

She caught her breath, and looked at him with a softer expression in her eyes.

'Ay, I'd like it fine, laddie.'

Magnus sank back in his seat, feeling a sudden peace stealing over him. Outside the wind continued to howl, but he did not listen to it. He could only hear Gran calling him laddie.